KU-422-795

Items on loan can be renewed by phone or Internet. Call 0845 230 3232 or visit our website.

Buckinghamshire
libraryservice
CULTURE AND LEARNING

www.buckscc.gov.uk/libraries

PUPPY FAT

Morris Gleitzman

First published in 1994
by Pan Macmillan Australia
This Large Print edition published by
BBC Audiobooks Ltd
by arrangement with
Macmillan Children's Books
2005

ISBN 1 4056 6060 0

British Library Cataloguing in Publication Data

Gleitzman, Morris
  Puppy fat.—Large print ed.
  1. Shipley, Keith (Fictitious character)—Juvenile
  fiction 2. Parents—Juvenile fiction 3. Children's
  stories 4. Large type books
  I. Title
  823.9'14[J]

ISBN-10: 1-4056-6060-0

Printed and bound in Great Britain by
Antony Rowe Ltd., Chippenham, Wiltshire

For Sophie and Ben

CHAPTER ONE

Keith stood at the front of the queue and sent an urgent message to the chicken nuggets and peas in his stomach. Relax, he told them. This isn't a big drama. I'm just putting a couple of ads in the local paper. No need to get worked up.

'Next,' said the woman behind the counter.

Keith took a deep breath, stepped forward and handed her the two forms.

She peered at them for ages.

Keith swallowed.

His mouth felt dry.

Suddenly the newspaper office had got very hot.

Perhaps someone wants to advertise a central heating system, thought Keith, and they've brought it in with them.

'I can't read this writing,' said the woman. 'What section?'

'Sorry?' said Keith.

'What section do you want to

advertise in? Toys? Sporting Equipment? Computers And Video Games?' The woman took her glasses off and polished them wearily on her cardigan. 'What are you advertising?'

'My parents,' said Keith.

The woman stopped polishing.

She peered at Keith for even longer than she had at the forms.

This is it, thought Keith. This is where she either chucks me out or she doesn't.

'Your parents,' said the woman.

'It's OK,' said Keith, 'they're separated.'

The woman put her glasses back on and squinted at the pieces of paper.

Keith leaned forward and took them back.

'Sorry about the writing,' he said. 'You'll recognise the words when I read them. Mrs Lambert at school always does.'

He took another deep breath and had a quick word with his blood. Listen, he told it, half of South London's in the queue behind us so I'd really appreciate you not rushing to my face and making it go red. Thanks.

'This first one's advertising my dad,' said Keith to the woman. He started reading, pointing to each word. 'Chef, 37½, non-smoker, only swears on motorways, very little dandruff, good in goal, wants to meet kind woman (no criminal record) to go out together and be friends.'

Keith paused in case any women in the queue wanted to fix up a date now and save him the 27p a word, extra for thick type.

No one did.

Never mind, thought Keith. People probably haven't got time for romance when they're trying to work out how much to ask for their lawn mower.

'This other one's advertising my mum,' he said to the counter woman, who was staring at him suspiciously.

He held the other form up so she could see the words.

'Council employee,' he read, 'only been 36 for a couple of weeks, very good at Monopoly, expert cuddler, never gets carsick, own TV, wants to meet kind man—'

'Excuse me,' interrupted the woman.

For a sec Keith thought she'd spotted a bloke in the queue who wanted to invite Mum to the pictures, but she hadn't.

'Did your parents write these adverts themselves?' asked the woman sternly.

'No,' said Keith quietly.

The woman's face grew even sterner.

'They would have done,' Keith added hurriedly, 'but they've been a bit depressed lately. We went to live in Australia to try and save their marriage, but it didn't work out and they've been in the dumps a bit since we got back.'

'I'm afraid we only accept Personals from the individuals concerned,' said the woman.

Keith sighed.

This was what he'd feared.

'Please,' he said. 'Just this once.'

'Sorry,' said the woman.

'Go on,' pleaded Keith. 'You'll be bringing happiness to two seriously depressed people.'

'Sorry,' said the woman.

'My best friend's coming from

4

Australia for a holiday,' said Keith. 'She's only here for eleven days.'

'What's that got to do with it?' asked the woman.

'Tracy can perk anyone up,' explained Keith, 'even people who are seriously depressed. Starting next Thursday she'll be here perking Mum and Dad up which'll be the perfect time for them to be getting romantic letters and meeting new people and falling in love and cheering up and being happy for the rest of their lives.'

'Sorry,' said the woman.

'Tracy's mum's coming too,' said Keith desperately. 'She's been married for eighteen years. She'll be able to help them sort through the letters and pick the good partners.'

'Sorry,' said the woman. 'Next.'

I bet you're not sorry, thought Keith bitterly as he turned away. I bet you're only doing the job for the cheap lawn mowers.

As he walked dejectedly out of the newspaper office he looked closely at the people in the queue to see if anyone was having second thoughts about asking Mum or Dad out.

No one was.

*　　　*　　　*

The glamorous countess gave the dashing cavalry officer a smouldering look. She walked slowly across the moonlit balcony, slipped her hand inside his tunic and pulled out a jar of instant coffee.

'Ridiculous,' said Mum, scowling at the TV. 'That woman hasn't got a bottom. And look at those ridiculous shoulders. She's got enough padding in there to stuff a car seat.'

Keith sighed and had another chocolate finger.

It was getting worse.

Only three months since Mum and Dad had split up and here was Mum spending every evening flopped in front of the telly in an old housecoat and bed socks, criticising the adverts and neglecting her waistline.

'Pass the fingers, love,' said Mum.

Keith sighed again.

Up until three months ago, she'd

been dead strict about chocolate fingers.

Two a day and ten on birthdays, that had been the rule.

Now it was a box a night.

And she didn't care how many he had, either.

Perhaps if I pretend I didn't hear, thought Keith, she'll forget she asked.

'Keith,' said Mum, 'use one of those chocolate fingers to clean the wax out of your ears and pass the rest to me please, love.'

Tragic, thought Keith sadly as he handed her the box. A clever woman who used to be really good at homework and Monopoly reduced to a lonely chocolate-guzzling vegetable.

But she could snap out of it, he knew she could.

All she needed was some help.

*   *   *

At Dad's place things weren't much better.

Dad was staring at a naked woman.

Keith stared too.

7

She looked exactly like Mrs Lambert.

It couldn't be.

A geography teacher wouldn't lie on a red velvet settee wearing only a tiara and a pair of green slippers and let someone do a painting of her.

Not if the painting was going to be shown on telly.

The image on the TV changed to the reporter's head.

'. . . eighteenth century Italian masterpiece,' the reporter was saying, 'sold for a record twenty-seven million pounds.'

'If I had twenty-seven million quid,' said Dad bitterly to the screen, 'I wouldn't blow it on an old painting, I'd get the cooker in the cafe overhauled.'

As Keith's eyes got used to the darkness in Dad's living room he saw that Dad was lying on the settee wearing only a knitted beanie and his striped pyjamas.

'Hello Keith,' he said without looking up. 'Didn't see you come in.'

'OK if I stay tonight?' said Keith.

'Course,' said Dad. 'Any time you

like, you know that.'

He swung his legs off the settee so Keith could sit down.

'Dad,' said Keith, 'do you feel like going bowling? I'll pay.'

Keith held his breath.

Think positive.

'Not tonight Keith,' said Dad. 'I'm settled here now.'

Keith sighed.

You've been settled there every night for the last three months, he thought sadly. Just as well this flat's over the cafe and the heat from the frying stops it getting damp or you'd have moss on your bum.

He sat down.

Dad stretched out again with his legs over Keith's knees.

Tragic, thought Keith. If anyone could see Dad now they'd think he was a victim of some tropical disease that makes you spend all your spare time watching telly. They wouldn't have a clue they were looking at a man who could score 120 at tenpin bowling and cook any sausage in the whole world without bursting the skin.

9

'Dennis Baldwin's dad met a film star at the bowling alley,' said Keith, 'and now they're married and living in Malibu.'

It wasn't true but he was desperate.

Dad didn't answer.

He was staring at the telly.

On the screen an Alsatian was driving a golf buggy.

Keith suddenly wanted to grab Dad and shake him and yell at him to pull himself together and get on with his life.

Instead he took a deep breath and calmed down.

Violence wouldn't solve anything.

Dad just needed some help.

*   *   *

Keith stood at the sink in the cafe and plunged a baked-bean-encrusted plate into the hot soapy water.

None of the baked beans moved.

They were like pebbles.

As Keith scrubbed at the pebbles with a piece of steel wool he pretended they were gall stones he'd removed from the stomach of the woman in the newspaper office.

'Thank you, oh, thank you,' he imagined her sobbing. 'You can put those ads in now if you like.'

'Don't need to,' he imagined himself replying airily as he took off his surgeon's gown. 'There are plenty of other places to advertise mums and dads?'

Telly, for example.

Or magazines.

Or the sides of buses.

Keith grinned as he imagined painting a huge picture of Mum and Dad on the side of a bus, including their phone numbers.

Then his face fell as he wondered how much London Transport would charge.

Thousands probably.

Keith tried to work out how long he'd take to earn thousands of quid in washing-up money at 5p a plate and 7p for saucepans.

His brain went soupier than the washing-up water.

What I need, thought Keith, is

somewhere cheap I can display a really attention-grabbing picture of Mum and Dad where it'll be seen by loads of people who aren't being distracted by lawn mower prices.

Suddenly he stopped scrubbing the plate.

Of course.

Why hadn't he thought of it before?

CHAPTER TWO

Keith peered through the keyhole into Dad's bathroom.

Come on Dad, he thought, stop moving about. Entries in the school art show close at lunchtime today.

Dad carried on having his morning cough in front of the mirror.

Bet the great painters of history didn't have this trouble, thought Keith as he watched Dad's body shake with each cough. Bet when the great painters of history painted people in the nude they didn't have to wait for the people's bottoms to stop wobbling.

Keith started on the background, squinting through the keyhole to check that he was mixing the right shade of Pond Green to match the bathroom wallpaper.

Bet the great painters of history didn't have to work kneeling down outside a bathroom door, either, thought Keith bitterly. Bet people were only too glad to take their clothes off for them.

Queued up to do it, probably.

Not like Dad.

'Paint me with my gear off?' he'd spluttered, nearly choking on his bedtime cuppa. 'Do you want to get us arrested?'

Keith had tried to explain that the great painters of history had most of their big successes doing people with no clothes on.

He'd reminded Dad about the twenty-seven million quid painting on telly.

But all Dad had said was, 'Give me twenty-seven million quid and I'll think about it.'

Keith had been tempted to tell Dad

why he wanted to do the painting, but he'd decided against it.

If Dad knew he was being advertised he'd get all tense and embarrassed.

Tense and embarrassed's no good, thought Keith as he brushed the Pond Green on to the thick paper. I've got to show Dad as he really is.

Warm-hearted.

Sensitive.

A whiz with fried foods.

Keith finished the background and peered through the keyhole again.

In front of the mirror Dad gave one last cough, then stopped.

After a bit, his bottom stopped wobbling.

And his tummy.

Then he sighed and his tummy sagged and his bottom drooped.

Tragic, thought Keith sadly.

And Dad only thirty-seven.

Wonder if the great painters of history had this problem? Wonder if Picasso's dad let himself go physically, after he split up with Picasso's mum?

Keith's heart sank as he watched Dad trying to arrange some wisps of hair over his bald patch.

Then Keith took a deep breath, told himself to think positive, squeezed out some Flesh Pink and got on with the job.

*　　　*　　　*

Keith stared at Mum's bathroom door.

No keyhole.

OK, he thought, don't panic. What would the great painters of history have done? Bathroom doors in fifteenth century Italy probably didn't have keyholes either, so Botticelli would have faced this problem a lot.

Keith crouched next to the door handle and peered at the crack of light between the door and the door frame.

The door wasn't bolted.

Keith put his painting stuff on the floor and listened.

He could hear Mum splashing in the bath, and the radio playing the sort of violin music that usually made him feel depressed.

Not today, though, because it was just what he needed to drown out any door squeaks.

Keith sent an urgent message to the batteries in Mum's radio.

Don't conk out, please.

Then he slowly turned the handle and pushed the door open a fraction.

He held his breath and waited for an indignant yell from Mum. That was the trouble with her flat being seventeen floors up, the draughts were something chronic.

Nothing.

She must have the heater on.

He peeked in.

Through the steam he could see Mum in the bath, eyes closed, chin on her chest, listening to the music.

He watched her sadly.

Even in the bath her posture was bad, shoulders slumped and sort of curled forward.

On her feet, which were resting on the end of the bath, he could see corns and bunions and other lumpy bits.

And the veins in her legs looked like a road map of somewhere that had purple roads.

Tragic.

16

And Mum only thirty-six.

Never mind, thought Keith, she's got a wonderful personality.

Think positive.

All I've got to do is make sure this painting captures her good points.

Her sense of humour.

Her loving nature.

Her talent for Monopoly.

Keith chose a brush and started on her feet.

*   *   *

'Hmmmm,' said Mr Browning, staring at the painting, 'interesting.'

Mr Browning didn't look very interested to Keith, he looked like he'd just eaten some varnish.

Keith reminded himself that Mr Browning always looked like that while he was thinking about a picture. Must be something art teachers learn as part of their training.

Keith glanced around the school hall and felt a tingle of excitement. The art show was filling up. Groups of people were arriving and staring with interest at the pictures on the walls, and they couldn't all be married.

Soon they'd be staring with interest at Mum and Dad.

'Title?' asked Mr Browning.

'It's got two titles,' said Keith. 'The left-hand side's called *Nude Dad With Frying Pan.*'

'Hmmmm,' said Mr Browning again.

'I made him nude,' said Keith hurriedly, 'cause the great painters of history had some of their biggest successes with nudes. The frying pan is to show he's a chef in a cafe. And to hide his rude bits.'

Keith felt his cheeks go hot.

He had an urgent word with his blood.

Go back down to my legs. Now.

'Hmmmm,' said Mr Browning. 'Very good use of colour, specially your dad's blue hair.'

Keith nodded.

He decided not to mention that it was actually a plastic shower cap he'd added to cover Dad's bald patch.

'What's the right-hand side called?' asked Mr Browning, shifting his gaze to

Mum in the bath.

'*Venus Soaking Her Corns*,' said Keith. 'Mum's name is actually Marge, but the great painters of history usually called their lady nudes Venus. Or Mona.'

'Hmmmm,' said Mr Browning. 'I like the way you've got the light falling across her shoulders like a cloak to remind us she's an historical figure.'

Keith nodded again and decided not to mention that it was actually a shower curtain he'd put in to hide Mum's bad posture.

'And having her playing Monopoly in the bath,' said Mr Browning. 'Very imaginative. She's a real-estate agent, is she?'

Keith shook his head. 'Parking inspector,' he said.

Mr Browning continued to look closely at Mum.

'Is that a phone number,' he asked, 'in soap suds, floating on the top of the water?'

Keith nodded and felt his heart speed up.

It was working.

Mr Browning was becoming fascinated by Mum's finer qualities.

'She's good at Scrabble, too,' said Keith. 'And cards.'

Then he remembered Mr Browning was married.

With triplets.

'But she hasn't got very good feet,' Keith said hurriedly.

Mr Browning smiled and glanced around the hall.

'You'd better lower your voice,' he said, 'in case she hears you.'

'She's not here,' said Keith. 'She's doing a late shift.'

'Well, your dad then,' said Mr Browning. 'Don't want him hearing you bad-mouthing your mum's feet.'

'Mum and Dad are separated,' said Keith. 'And Dad's doing dinners at the cafe till nine.'

Mr Browning looked at the painting again, and then at Keith.

He seemed lost for words, which Keith hadn't ever seen before with Mr Browning.

He didn't even say 'Hmmmm.'

'Well done, Keith,' he said finally.

'It's a good effort. Keep it up. I hope you won't stop painting just because term's finished.'

Then he turned and went to look at another picture.

Keith pretended to go and look at another picture too.

Best not hang around mine, he thought. People get nervous copying down phone numbers from paintings when the artist's standing there watching them.

He glanced around the hall.

They couldn't all be mums and dads.

There must be some single people.

Keith tried to work out which ones were unattached, separated, divorced, widowed, abandoned, or had partners in jail for life.

It wasn't easy.

Then, with a jolt, he realized some people were looking at his painting.

Two women by themselves and a man by himself.

Keith liked the look of all of them, and he knew Mum and Dad would too.

He strained to hear what they were saying.

'Dodgy legs,' said one of the women, pointing to Dad.

They both sniggered.

'Hers aren't much better,' said the man, pointing to Mum.

The three of them walked away laughing.

Tragic, thought Keith. Fancy thinking the most important thing about a person is whether the veins in their legs stick out a bit.

He looked around again.

The hall was even more crowded now.

People were arriving all the time.

Keith relaxed.

He could tell that lots of them were sensitive, mature single people who knew that leg veins weren't really very important at all.

*   *   *

Keith lay in bed and stared into the darkness and tried to stop seeing leg veins.

He couldn't.

'Dodgy legs,' said the school-hall

voices in his head.

And 'Yuk, look at that tummy.'

And 'I've seen better looking skin on a potato.'

And 'Who's that in the bath, the Hunchback of Notre Dame?'

And 'Fire! Fire!'

Keith smiled grimly in the darkness.

That would have shut them up.

If he'd ripped his painting off the wall and grabbed Mr Browning's matches and set fire to it.

That would have stopped them saying unkind things about other people's bodies.

They'd have all stood round speechless and watched the flames gobble up Mum and Dad.

Then they'd have turned to Keith, stunned. 'Why?' they'd have asked him. 'Why have you destroyed your work of art?'

'I've gone off it,' he'd have replied casually. 'There was a mistake in the bathmat.'

Keith sighed in the dark.

The real mistake, he thought sadly, was the whole idea.

Thinking anyone could feel romantic about two people with dodgy legs, wobbly bottoms, saggy tummies, bad posture, blotchy skin and tired hair.

Keith switched his bedside light on and stared up at the tropical rainforest painted on his bedroom ceiling and tried not to think about Mum and Dad and how they were going to be lonely and unhappy for the rest of their lives because they'd let themselves go physically.

He concentrated on the swirls of colour above his head, the happy orchids and the cheerful parrots and the carefree waterfalls, and soon he was thinking about Tracy.

She'll be here in a week, he told himself, and we'll have heaps of fun and I won't have to think about Mum and Dad's problems once.

CHAPTER THREE

Hope I've remembered everything she likes, thought Keith as he hurried down the street.

He read through his shopping list again:

Beetroot (tinned)
Vegemite (large)
Pineapple (fresh)
Coconut (whole)
Peanuts (boiled)
Sugar cane (unprocessed)
Bubblegum (mango)

Right, he thought. Start with the hardest. Where am I going to find mango bubblegum in South London?

'Hello Keith,' said a voice behind him.

Before he could turn round, a hand had snatched the list.

Keith sighed.

Mitch Wilson.

'Why would anyone boil peanuts?' said Mitch, looking up from the piece of paper.

Keith snatched it back and glared at him.

'Is it to kill the germs?' said Mitch.

Keith took a deep breath.

Sometimes the only way to shake off pesky ten-year-olds was to answer them, specially when they were taller than you.

'In Queensland,' said Keith, 'boiled peanuts are regarded as a delicacy.'

'This isn't Queensland,' said Mitch, 'it's England.'

Tragic, thought Keith. The body of a thirteen-year-old and the mind of a whelk.

'My best friend's arriving from Australia on Thursday,' said Keith. 'I'm getting some Australian food in for her so she'll feel at home.'

'My dad says when foreigners come here they should eat English food,' said Mitch.

'She will eat English food,' said Keith.

'So why are you getting her all this Australian stuff?' said Mitch.

'She'll eat it as well,' said Keith. 'She's a big eater.'

As they turned the corner he wondered if there was a better way to shake off pesky ten-year-olds.

Like whacking them round the head

with a shopping bag.

Then he stopped.

Parked in the street in front of him was an ambulance with its back doors open.

A small crowd of people were watching two ambulance officers carry a stretcher out of a house.

'Look,' Mitch excitedly, 'someone's hurt themselves.'

Keith looked at the house to see if it was anyone he knew.

It wasn't.

He decided to let Mitch do the gawking for both of them.

Before he could get past, the crowd stepped back to let the stretcher through, blocking the pavement.

Under the blanket covering the stretcher Keith could see the outline of a person's body.

'He was only fifty-eight,' said a woman in the crowd. 'Poor thing.'

'Bet it was his heart,' said another woman.

'No,' said the first woman. 'Lost the will to live, more like. Mrs Mellish was killed by a bread van eight years ago.

27

Poor Mr Mellish has been on his own ever since.'

'Kill you stone dead, loneliness can,' said a man.

Keith stared at the stretcher.

A dreadful feeling was growing in his guts.

What if they were right?

What if loneliness could kill people stone dead?

Even people who were only thirty-six and thirty-seven and who were perfectly healthy apart from a bit of sagging and wobbling?

The people in the crowd chewed their lips while the ambulance officers heaved the body on the stretcher into the back of the ambulance.

Keith realized his chest had gone tight.

His eyes were hot and prickly.

Mitch Wilson was staring at him.

'Did you know him?' asked Mitch.

Keith turned away, blinking back tears.

There were some things you couldn't expect a ten-year-old to understand, even one who was abnormally tall for

28

his age.

*　　　*　　　*

Keith squeezed his way through the crowded market.

This is ridiculous, he thought.

Here's Mum and Dad doomed to an early grave and I'm off buying tropical fruit.

He tried not to think about it.

Mum and Dad's bodies being carried out on their lonely settees while the neighbours muttered about how tragically young they were.

A sad-faced minister at the funeral saying how their lonely deaths could have been avoided if only they'd done something about their leg veins.

Keith sent a stern message to his brain.

Stop it.

Concentrate on the shopping.

He peered through the jostling crowd at the various stalls.

There must be pineapples or coconuts here somewhere, he thought.

Then he saw it.

A bundle of long greeny-gold sticks leaning against a van behind a stall.

Sugar cane.

As Keith pushed his way over to the stall he remembered the first time he'd chewed into a sweet, juicy length of sugar cane.

At Tracy's place in Orchid Cove.

Tracy's Aunty Bev had given it to him and while they'd chewed she'd told him all about her work as a beautician.

Keith smiled as he remembered Aunty Bev's huge plastic parrot earrings and how they'd jiggled each time she'd given Tracy some beauty advice.

Tracy had rolled her eyes a lot, specially when Aunty Bev had explained that a kid with Tracy's fair skin would look much better cane-toad hunting in a lighter shade of gumboot.

But she'd had to admit that Aunty Bev's motto was a good one.

'If you want to get noticed, dazzle the punters.' Even though the market was full of people yelling about how fresh their caulies were and how their spuds were lovely, Keith could hear

Aunty Bev now in his head, as clearly as he had in Tracy's back yard under the brilliant tropical blue sky and the black smoke from Tracy's dad's barbecue.

'Dazzle the punters.'

Keith stopped pushing his way toward the sugar cane.

An idea was sizzling in his head like one of Tracy's dad's sausages.

Of course.

The mistake he'd made at the art show was to paint Mum and Dad the way they actually were.

Wobbly bottoms and dodgy legs.

That wasn't going to dazzle anyone.

What he should be doing was painting Mum and Dad the way they could be if they pulled their fingers out and got a grip on themselves and started to think positive.

Keith gave a huge grin.

'Thanks, Aunty Bev,' he said.

Then he turned and pushed and wriggled his way out of the market as fast as he could.

*   *   *

31

'A mural?' said Mr Dodd.

Come on, thought Keith desperately, you own the biggest hardware shop for about six streets, you must know what a mural is.

'It's a large painting on a wall or other vertical surface,' said Keith.

'I know what a mural is,' said Mr Dodd, following Keith out into the street, 'I'm just not sure if I want one.'

He put his hands into the pockets of his dustcoat and looked doubtfully up at the side wall of his shop.

'It'll brighten up that dirty brickwork no end,' said Keith.

Mr Dodd frowned.

'I was planning to rent that wall out,' he said. 'For advertising.'

Keith sent an urgent message to his brain.

Think.

'That's exactly what my mural will be doing,' said Keith. 'Advertising.'

Mr Dodd thought about this.

Keith saw a glint of interest appear in his eyes.

'You mean advertising my paint?'

said Mr Dodd.'

'Um . . . yes,' said Keith hastily. 'That's it. Advertising your paint.'

Mr Dodd's eyes gleamed and he started tracing words in the air with his hands. 'Dodds Hardware For All Your Paint Needs. Expert Advice. Lowest Prices.' He grinned excitedly at Keith. 'Good, eh?'

Think faster, Keith begged his brain.

'Actually, Mr Dodd,' he said, 'I was thinking of something a bit different.'

'Rock Bottom Prices?' said Mr Dodd.

'A painting of this street,' said Keith, 'except instead of doing the houses like they are now—boring front doors and off-white window frames and dirty brick walls—I'll do them in really good colours so people can see how great their places would look if they bought some paint from you and did them up.'

He stopped, out of breath.

Mr Dodd had gone thoughtful again.

'And you wouldn't want any money?' he said. 'Just the paint?'

Keith nodded.

'Are you any good?' asked Mr Dodd.

Keith unrolled the paintings he'd brought.

He watched anxiously as Mr Dodd scrutinized the first one.

'That's my friend Tracy on her roof in Australia chasing cane toads,' said Keith.

'Why's she got green hair?' said Mr Dodd.

'It's a shower cap,' said Keith. 'You have to wear protective headgear when you're chasing cane toads.'

Mr Dodd looked at the next painting.

'That was the fish-and-chip shop we had in Queensland,' said Keith.

Mr Dodd was frowning.

Keith held his breath.

'Nice colour,' said Mr Dodd. 'Make sure you use plenty of that Tropical Mango Gloss in the mural.'

Keith felt like hugging Mr Dodd, but he managed to control himself.

Mr Dodd tapped his finger on the painting, pointing to where Tracy was doing a handstand outside the fish-and-chip shop.

'Don't have too many people in the

34

mural,' said Mr Dodd, 'they'll obscure the paintwork on the houses.'

'I won't,' said Keith. 'Just two.'

'And no scruffs,' said Mr Dodd. 'Make them presentable.'

'Don't worry,' said Keith happily, 'they'll be very presentable.'

CHAPTER FOUR

'It's Disneyland,' said Mitch Wilson.

'It's a Nintendo game,' said Dennis Baldwin.

'It's a row of dolls houses seen through the infra-red night scope of an F-111 fighter plane,' said Rami Smith.

'Blimey,' said Eric Cox. 'It's this street. Why would you paint a street on a wall?'

Keith sighed.

Bet the great painters of history didn't have to put up with this, he thought. Bet when the great painters of history were risking their lives up a ladder painting a mural they had armed guards to stop the general public making distracting comments.

'Hey, Shipley,' Eric Cox yelled, 'you've got the colours all wrong.'

Keith tried to glare down at them, but seeing the ground so far away made him feel giddy and sick. He gripped the ladder tighter and concentrated on the Vivid Purple he was using for number 21's windowsills.

'Number 19 hasn't got a green and pink front door,' yelled Mitch Wilson.

'Number 21 hasn't got red and purple windows,' yelled Dennis Baldwin.

'They will have,' said Rami Smith, 'after the F-111 fires its heat-seeking missiles and splatters the whole street with blood and guts.'

Keith sighed again.

*   *   *

'Nice,' said Mr Dodd. 'Very nice. That Custard Yellow on number 23's front fence looks a treat. And that's a knockout idea, giving number 25 Mediterranean Blue and Atlantic Green striped guttering.'

'Thanks,' said Keith.

He didn't look down, partly because he didn't want to get giddy again and partly because he needed all his concentration for the Tropical Mango TV aerial he was giving number 27. TV aerials were always fiddly, even on a painting as huge as this one.

'Keith,' said Mr Dodd, 'don't forget to use some Suntan Gold. I overordered on Suntan Gold and I want to try and shift it before stocktaking.'

'Don't worry Mr Dodd,' said Keith, waving his brush, 'I'll be using plenty of Suntan Gold.'

'Good one,' said Mr Dodd. 'I'm closing for lunch now. Why don't you take a break? You've been up that ladder for hours. You must be exhausted.'

'I'm fine, thanks,' said Keith, hoping his aching arm didn't drop off there and then in front of Mr Dodd. 'I want to get this finished before dark.'

Keith almost had second thoughts as he heard Mr Dodd locking up the shop.

A fried-egg sandwich would be nice.

But he gritted his teeth and carried on.

Bet the great painters of history didn't knock off for lunch, he thought. Specially not when they'd almost got to the most important part of a picture.

He sent a message to his aching arms and his aching neck and his aching back and his aching legs.

Stop aching.

Then he finished number 27's aerial, gave them a Tropical Mango front door, wiped some drips off number 23's front fence, and touched up a couple of places he'd missed on the road.

And then it was time.

At last.

For the part he'd been waiting for.

Mum and Dad.

Suddenly he was so excited he hardly felt his aching bits at all as he climbed down the ladder to get the tin of Suntan Gold.

*　　　*　　　*

'Mmmm,' said Mr Browning. 'Interesting.'

Keith waited anxiously for him to say more.

Can't be easy being an art teacher, thought Keith. You pop out for some groceries in the school holidays, come round a corner with your shopping bags, and there's one of your pupils finishing off a twenty-foot painting.

'Title?' asked Mr Browning.

'*Dazzle The Punters*,' said Keith.

Mr Browning gave him a look, then crossed the road, stared at the mural from a distance and came back over.

'Excellent use of colour,' said Mr Browning.

'Thanks,' said Keith. 'Mr Dodd actually chose the colours.'

'And very good brushwork,' continued Mr Browning, gazing up at the wall, 'specially on the two people standing in the middle of the road in their underwear.'

'Thanks,' said Keith. 'Actually they're swimming costumes.'

He watched proudly as Mr Browning studied Dad's muscular Suntan Gold legs, non-saggy Suntan Gold lower buttocks, flat Suntan Gold stomach, broad Suntan Gold chest and smiling Suntan Gold face, and Mum's cascading Goddess Blonde ringlets with Suntan Gold highlights, erect Suntan Gold shoulders, non-droopy Suntan Gold hips, smooth Suntan Gold legs and bunion-free Suntan Gold feet.

'A superbly-balanced composition,' said Mr Browning, 'particularly the way the frying pan full of sausages in the man's hand is exactly the same size as the Monopoly board under the woman's arm.'

'Thanks,' said Keith.

'Next term,' said Mr Browning, 'remind me to show you a book about the French artist Magritte. He did a lot of paintings like this.'

Keith opened his mouth to ask if Magritte had any luck saving his mum and dad's lives.

Then he decided he'd rather not know.

'Keith,' said Mr Browning, 'do your parents know you've done this?'

'No,' said Keith, 'not yet.'

*   *   *

'Amazing,' said Mum.

'Incredible,' said Dad.

'You did all this by yourself?' said Mum.

Keith nodded.

He couldn't understand why he was feeling so giddy.

He wasn't up the ladder, he was standing on the pavement with Mum and Dad and Mr Dodd.

Then he realized he was holding his breath.

He took a lungful of air without taking his eyes off Mum and Dad, and his ears tingled, partly from the oxygen and partly from the excitement.

It was working.

Mum and Dad were fascinated by themselves as big, tanned, fit, handsome, happy people.

Mum's shoulders were already looking straighter inside her parking inspector's uniform, and Dad's bottom, sticking out through the back of his cafe apron, was already looking firmer.

Keith could see the thoughts going through their minds.

Exercise, Dad was thinking. Hair transplant. Suntan lamp.

Perm, Mum was thinking. New swimsuit. Get my feet done.

'Great houses,' said Dad. 'Who are those weird people?'

Keith looked over his shoulder.

There was no one there.

He realized Dad meant the people in the mural.

'Those,' said Mr Dodd, 'are people who've discovered that repainting the house cuts down on maintenance so much they're left with bags of time for a holiday in Spain. Isn't that right, Keith?'

Suddenly Keith was having trouble breathing.

'It's a joke,' said Mum. 'Keith's making fun of all those ads for cars and chocolate bars and perfume that are full of people the rest of us couldn't ever possibly hope to look like. It's very funny, Keith. I like it.'

Keith was suddenly feeling so giddy he had to hold on to a lamppost.

42

Why couldn't they recognize themselves?

They weren't that different in the mural.

Their faces were the same.

And their hands.

Plus they had their phone numbers written on their tummies in blockout cream.

Stay calm, he told himself.

All that's happened is that Mum and Dad's eyesight is going.

'Lovely brushwork,' said Dad, 'but why didn't you take it right into the corners?' He pointed up at the brickwork still showing at the top corners of the wall.

Forget that idea, thought Keith miserably.

There couldn't be anything wrong with Dad's eyesight if he could see the tiny bits Keith hadn't been able to reach without falling off the ladder and being killed.

'That's a very imaginative way of signing your painting, love,' said Mum, pointing up at the tummies. 'Putting your phone numbers instead of your name.'

Keith sent a frantic message to his tear ducts.

Stay closed.

'I think it's great,' said Mum, ruffling his hair.

Keith noticed sadly that her shoulders weren't that straight after all.

'So do I,' said Dad, his bottom wobbling inside his trousers while he shook Keith by the hand.

Keith took a deep breath and started clearing away the paint tins while Mr Dodd took Mum and Dad inside to show them a new paint for toilets that had a built-in air freshener.

Tragic, thought Keith.

They're so used to being saggy and wobbly they can't even recognize their real selves.

He took another deep breath.

It'll be fine, he told himself.

As soon as passers-by start seeing the mural, Mum and Dad's phones will be ringing hot with invitations to the pub and the pictures and they'll have to start thinking about suntan lamps and hairdos then.

Keith looked up at the mural.

Mum and Dad's Suntan Gold faces grinned down at him from the wall.

Good one, Keith said to them.

Think positive.

CHAPTER FIVE

Keith sent an urgent message to Mum's phone.

Ring.

The phone sat on the sideboard and ignored him.

Keith gave it a pleading look.

Please.

The phone stayed silent.

Keith stood up and paced around the room. It was a small room, so after only six paces he was back on the settee.

This is ridiculous, he thought.

Nearly half a day that mural's been up and not a single call.

The phone must be broken.

He went over and picked up the hand piece. The dial tone buzzed in his ear. He put it down quickly in case someone was trying to call.

They weren't.

After another pace around the room, it hit him.

Of course.

Must be a fault at the exchange.

Someone down at the exchange must have plugged an electric kettle and a three-bar heater into the same double adaptor and blown all the circuits.

At this very moment in every phone box within a two mile radius of the mural there was probably a mature-age single person frantically trying to ring Mum or Dad, not realizing the phones in the whole area were out.

Keith grabbed his jacket.

He'd go round all the phone boxes and be back here with a pile of invitations for Mum before she got home from work.

At the front door his stomach gave a rumble and he realized he was starving.

It's all this nervous tension, he thought, it's burning up my breakfast at a faster than usual rate. Must be careful to keep my energy levels up.

He went into the kitchen and pulled open the chocolate finger drawer.

It was empty.

Strange, he thought.

He rummaged through the cupboard where Mum kept all the new groceries.

No chocolate fingers there either.

Or in the cereal cupboard.

Or in any of the jars.

Or in the oven.

Keith's guts suddenly felt even emptier than before.

Time was running out.

When a person lost her taste for chocolate fingers, the end couldn't be far away.

*　　　*　　　*

'Thursday,' Dad shouted as Keith walked into the cafe.

Keith stared.

A jab of excitement ran through him.

Dad was at the stove in a haze of blue smoke, with a pan of sausages in one hand and the phone in the other.

'Thursday at the latest,' shouted Dad.

At last, thought Keith. A woman enquiring how long Dad'll need to get his body into shape.

'Not too much fat,' Dad yelled above the sizzling of the sausages.

That's right, thought Keith, be positive.

Dad hung up.

'If that Len Tufnell doesn't start delivering my pork chops on time,' he said, 'I'm getting a new butcher.'

Keith suddenly felt very weary.

'You look pooped,' said Dad. 'What have you been doing with yourself?'

'Nothing much,' said Keith.

He didn't feel like going into detail about how he'd just been to every phone box this side of Woolwich, and how they'd all been empty except one and how the person inside it had told him to get lost or she'd set her dog on him.

'Dad,' said Keith hopefully, 'have you had any other phone calls this morning?'

Dad thought while he made a sausage sandwich.

'Just the wholesaler,' he said,

handing the sandwich to Keith, 'and an order for six takeaway egg and bacon rolls.Why, were you trying to ring?'

Keith shook his head and sat down at a table and stared at the sandwich. He wasn't hungry any more.

Why wasn't the mural working?

He'd made sure all the paint was waterproof so it wouldn't run in the rain.

The phone numbers were right, he'd double-checked.

Keith sighed.

I should have given Mum a bigger chest and Dad bigger leg muscles, he thought gloomily.

Then Mr Kristos, the owner of the cafe, came in for his liver and onions.

Keith noticed that as Dad served them up he didn't pop a bit of onion into his mouth like he usually did.

That's it, thought Keith.

Dad's a goner too.

When a person loses interest in fried onions, he's pretty much lost interest in life.

'Keith,' said Mr Kristos, coming and sitting at Keith's table, 'that painting

49

you done on that wall. Exquisite.'

'Thanks,' said Keith sadly.

'A masterpiece,' continued Mr Kristos through a mouthful of liver. 'Just one thing puzzles me. Why did you put your mum and dad's phone numbers on the stomachs of two bodybuilders?'

Keith opened his mouth to explain, but he felt too weary.

'Don't take offence,' said Mr Kristos. 'If it's art, just say so.'

'It's art,' said Keith, wondering if a person's eyesight could be damaged by eating too much liver.

What other explanation could there be for Mr Kristos not recognizing Dad in the mural, a man he saw every day at least once and sometimes up to eight times if the stove was playing up?

Unless . . .

Keith stared at Mr Kristos.

Suddenly it all made sense.

Of course.

That's why the mural wasn't working.

Mr Kristos and everyone else in the district were so used to Mum and Dad being wobbly and saggy they couldn't recognize Mum and Dad's real selves either. To them Dad was just the quiet bloke with the unfortunate bottom who cooked their bacon rolls, and Mum was just the poor soul with the tragic legs who gave their cars parking tickets.

But not for much longer, thought Keith happily.

It'll all change once Tracy arrives.

Once she starts perking Mum and Dad up, and they get a grip on themselves and suck their tummies in and pull their shoulders back and start smiling, people will start recognizing them in the mural and the invitations will come flooding in.

'No offence?' said Mr Kristos anxiously.

'None taken,' said Keith with a grin.

He bit hungrily into his sandwich.

'Oops,' said Dad from behind the counter, 'just remembered. There was another call this morning. Mrs Smith from the newsagents. She's got a fax for you from Tracy.'

*   *   *

Keith stood in the newsagents and read the fax for the third time.

Perhaps he'd got it wrong the first two times.

Perhaps he'd missed out some words.

Perhaps it wasn't terrible news after all and the brick he could feel in his guts would vanish.

Dear Keith, he read.

Something real crook's happened. A squall hit Dad's boat and turned it over and Dad tore half his ligaments. They sewed him up, but now he's in bed and Mum doesn't want to leave him cause he's already hurt himself once reaching for the comfort bucket.

So we can't come next week.

Poop. Poop. Poop. Poop. Poop. Poop.

Life can be a real mongrel, eh? First German measles, now this. Mum reckons we can come at Chrissie. That's another four months! I'll go mental. At this rate we'll be fifty before I get there. You'll be fat and bald and I won't recognize you.

Write soon, love Tracy.

PS. The prognosis for Dad is a complete recovery except for the boat.

There should be a law, thought Keith bitterly, to stop people taking small fishing boats out into North Queensland waters when the weather was changeable and their daughters were about to make important overseas trips to see best friends who were counting on them.

Keith realized Mrs Smith and Rami were staring at him from behind the counter.

'Are you all right, Keith?' asked Mrs Smith, concerned, twisting her sari anxiously in her fingers.

Keith nodded and tried to smile.

No point in upsetting her.

Rami held out Keith's change.

Keith took it.

'What does prognosis mean?' asked Rami.

Mrs Smith gave him a clip round the ear.

'It's when the doctors tell you you're

going to be OK,' said Keith. 'Or dead in a couple of months.'

He hurried out of the shop before Mrs Smith could ask him how Mum and Dad were.

*   *   *

Keith peered into the darkness.

The street lamp he was standing under was broken and the moon was behind a cloud and he couldn't see for sure if it was the right place or not.

He sent an urgent message to his eyes.

Please.

Try harder.

I don't want to break into the wrong house.

Keith took a couple of steps closer to the dark windows looming in front of him and suddenly a pain shot through his right hand.

Something had stabbed him in the knuckle.

He couldn't see if his hand was bleeding, so he gave it a suck just in case. His tongue felt the sharp end of a splinter. He crouched down and pulled it out.

In front of his face was a gate post.

Keith could just make out a jagged slash of new wood where the paint had been scraped off.

He remembered how two days ago he and Mitch Wilson had seen the ambulance men accidentally give the gatepost a thump with the stretcher as they carried the body out to the ambulance.

This was it.

The dead man's house.

Keith hurried along the street, counting the houses all the way to the corner. Then he ran round the corner and along the back alley, counting the houses again till he got to the dead man's back gate.

He leant against the gate and closed his eyes and sent an urgent message.

Sorry about this Mr . . . um . . .

He realized he couldn't remember the dead man's name.

Mr Milton?

Mr Stannish?

Mr Mellish, that was it.

Sorry about this Mr Mellish, said Keith silently, but I'm desperate. Tracy can't come now and this is the only other thing I can think of. Sorry.

He took a deep breath and clambered over the gate.

He hit the ground on the other side, slipped on the cold damp grass, picked himself up and ran towards the house.

He crouched at the back door, panting.

The windows at the back of the house were dark too.

Keith strained to hear if any sounds were coming from inside.

Nothing.

OK, he thought, the key.

He felt under the mat.

Nothing.

In the darkness he could make out some flowerpots next to the back step.

He felt inside them.

Behind them.

Under them.

Nothing.

Come on, he thought, everyone hides a backdoor key somewhere.

He groped around the other side of

the step, feeling for an old gardening shoe like Uncle Derek and Aunty Joyce used.

There wasn't one.

Just an empty milk bottle which toppled off the step and smashed loudly.

Keith froze.

He waited for all the neighbours who'd gawked at the body on the stretcher to come rushing out of their houses, and grab him and drag him off to the police station where he'd be charged with breaking and entering.

'I wasn't really breaking and entering, officer,' Keith rehearsed in his head, 'I was just trying to find out how Mr Mellish died. Whether it really was from loneliness or whether it was from something else like drink or bad diet or radiation from a leaky microwave. There are two lives at stake. Three if you count me worrying myself to death.'

After several rehearsals Keith realized he was still alone in the dark with his eardrums pounding.

When they'd stopped, he began

carefully feeling around for a key again.

Then he heard it.

Coming from inside the house.

A high-pitched wail.

It was very faint, but Keith knew as soon as it started that it wasn't a door creaking or a microwave leaking or the wind in a plug hole.

It was somebody crying.

Somebody or something.

A thin, eerie, mournful sound.

Keith's eardrums started pounding again.

He had a stern word with himself, reminding himself that he'd been around and he knew that ghosts were just a figment of the imagination.

He tried to swallow but the inside of his mouth felt dry and woolly like the blanket that had covered Mr Mellish's body.

The wailing was the saddest thing Keith had ever heard.

A thought slipped into his mind.

What if . . .

It was crazy so he waited for it to go away.

It didn't.

What if, he thought, the wailing is Mr Mellish trying to tell me he did die of loneliness and I mustn't give up trying to save Mum and Dad from a similar fate?

Keith realized he was shaking all over.

He had an even sterner word with himself, reminding himself that he hadn't believed in ghosts for over two years.

He listened to the wailing again.

Then he turned and ran for the back gate as fast as he could.

*   *   *

Keith lay on his bed at Dad's place.

He could feel his heart trying to jump out of his chest, partly from the running, partly from Mr Mellish's wailing, but mostly from the brilliant idea he'd had on the way home.

When his hands had stopped shaking, he found a pen and wrote a fax.

Dear Tracy,
Sorry about your dad. And the boat. But don't give up. Think positive. Somebody else could come with you.

My suggestion is Aunty Bev. She's single, self-employed and has a very positive attitude to life. I bet when she finds out your mum's ticket is up for grabs, she'll jump at the chance.

Tell her that once she's here she won't have to pay for any meals and Mum will make sure she doesn't get any parking tickets.

Don't give up. It's a matter of life or death. (I'll explain when you get here.)
Love, Keith.

Then he flopped back on to the bed and crossed his fingers very hard and hoped that Aunty Bev was open to new challenges in her work as a beautician.

*   *   *

The reply came two days later.

Dear Keith,
Ripper! Aunty Bev has said yes!

60

Mum says I can come! See you Thursday (same flight). Ripper!

Love Tracy.

PS. Aunty Bev can be a real pain sometimes, but I'm hoping travel will broaden her mind.

Keith stood in the newsagents and felt the brick in his guts melt away.

He realized Mrs Smith and Rami were smiling at him from behind the counter.

'What does ripper mean?' asked Rami.

Mrs Smith gave him a clip round the ear.

'It's an Australian word,' grinned Keith. 'It means everything's going to be OK.'

CHAPTER SIX

'Come on, Keith,' yelled Dad. 'Shake a leg. The plane lands in an hour.'

'Nearly ready,' shouted Keith.

He stopped and listened and heard

Dad down in the cafe stirring sugar into a cuppa.

Good, thought Keith, that gives me at least another five minutes.

Now, where are those baked beans?

I know.

The wardrobe.

Keith pulled open the doors of his wardrobe and ran his eyes over the cartons stacked inside.

Peas.

Spaghetti.

Marmalade.

No baked beans.

Keith dropped to the floor and lifted the edge of his bedspread and peered under his bed.

As his eyes got used to the gloom, the printing on the sides of the boxes became clearer.

Corned beef.

Apricot halves.

Baked beans.

Good one, thought Keith. He ticked baked beans off his list.

'Keith,' said Dad, 'we're going to be late.'

Keith looked up.

Dad was standing in the doorway with a steaming mug in one hand and a bacon sandwich in the other.

'What are you doing?' he asked.

'Just stocktaking,' said Keith, standing up.

Dad looked wearily at the cartons piled up around the room, sighed, and sat down on some boxes of fruit salad in heavy syrup.

Keith watched his mouth droop.

There were some lines at the corners Keith hadn't seen before.

'Not a great set-up, is it, sleeping in a storeroom?' said Dad. 'Wish I could afford a place with a room of your own, but I can't.'

'I don't mind,' said Keith.

'You're a good kid,' said Dad, 'but be honest, this isn't as good as your room at Mum's, is it?'

Keith sent an urgent message to his brain.

Make Dad feel better.

'It's very similar,' said Keith. 'Mum keeps her spare chocolate fingers under my bed. Well, she used to.'

It wasn't true, but he hoped it'd help.

'If you want me to shift some more of this stuff into my room, I will,' said Dad quietly. 'If I put the Irish stew on top of my wardrobe . . .'

'Dad,' interrupted Keith, 'I wasn't making a list for that. I was just checking we've got enough food for Tracy. I like staying with you.'

Dad's drooping mouth slowly straightened itself.

'Oh,' he said. 'Right.' Then he grinned. 'What was it Tracy used to say? "I'm so hungry I could eat the fingers off a goat"?'

'Fish,' said Keith, grinning too. 'I could eat the fingers off a fish.'

'That's it,' said Dad. 'OK, we'd better get out to that airport before she has a go at the luggage scales. Scales. Fish. Get it?'

Keith realized he hadn't heard Dad make a joke for months.

Amazing, he thought as he followed Dad out of the room. Tracy's not even here yet and she's perking him up already.

And as for those lines at the corner of his mouth, I won't have to worry about those any more.

Not once Aunty Bev gets her hands on them.

*   *   *

Keith stood at the barrier on tiptoe and strained for a glimpse of Tracy among the arriving passengers.

He couldn't see her.

For a horrible moment he had a vision of Tracy and Aunty Bev under arrest at Singapore airport because Aunty Bev's parrot earrings had set off the metal detector. Then he remembered they were plastic. He wondered if Aunty Bev had many fillings.

'G'day Keith.'

That familiar voice.

His heart did a backflip and he turned and there was Tracy coming towards him, grinning and waving behind a trolley piled with luggage.

Keith felt his own grin nearly splitting his cheeks.

Even his insides were grinning.

'G'day Tracy,' he said.

65

She hadn't changed a bit. Same fair hair, same tanned face, same pink patches where the brown was peeling off.

'I didn't reckon the plane was ever gunna get here,' said Tracy. 'I thought the pilot had fallen asleep in the movie and missed the turning at Bombay.'

Same old Tracy, thought Keith happily.

Except something was different.

It took Keith a moment to realize what it was.

He looked down at her feet to see if she was giving herself a ride on the trolley.

No, her feet were on the ground.

Blimey, thought Keith, she's almost as tall as Mitch Wilson.

He stepped closer to her, amazed.

Five months ago she could have chased cane toads with six green shower caps on her head and still been shorter than him.

Now, without even one, she was the same height.

And he was wearing really thick socks.

'What are you staring at?' said Tracy, still grinning. 'Have I got ink on my teeth? While we were landing I got a bit excited and chewed the sick bag.'

'Sorry,' said Keith, stepping back, 'just getting used to seeing you again.'

No point in embarrassing her.

Anyway, he thought, it's probably just temporary. Some people's feet swell on long flights, with other people it must be their spinal fluid. She'll be back to normal in a couple of hours.

'Where's Aunty Bev?' he asked.

He'd just realized with a jab of alarm she wasn't there.

'Dunno,' said Tracy. 'Maybe customs shot her.'

Keith looked anxiously towards the customs exit.

No sign of her.

Just a glamorous international model in a pink tracksuit probably coming back from starring in an instant coffee commercial in Jamaica or somewhere.

'Tracy,' said the glamorous international model, 'I asked you to wait for me while I was in the ladies.'

Keith saw with a jolt that the glamorous international model was wearing plastic parrot earrings.

'Sorry, Aunty Bev,' said Tracy.

Keith realized his mouth was hanging open.

'G'day, Keith,' said Aunty Bev, 'good to see you again mate.'

'G-g'day,' stammered Keith.

She shook his hand and the movement made her blonde wavy hair bounce up and down.

No wonder I didn't recognize her, thought Keith.

At Tracy's barbecue her hair had been black and Keith was pretty sure that hadn't just been the soot from the sausages.

He tried not to stare.

It was incredible.

All the other passengers had got off the plane looking like they'd just spent twenty-four hours in with the luggage. Keith had never seen so many puffy eyes and rumpled clothes and saggy bottoms and flattened hairdos.

There wasn't a single part of Aunty Bev that was puffy, rumpled, saggy or

68

flattened. Her shiny red high-heeled shoes weren't even scuffed.

'Is your dad here?' she asked.

Keith struggled to tear his eyes from Aunty Bev's face, which looked like it had been painted by one of those great painters of history who specialized in painting faces without a single crease, wrinkle, line, pimple or droopy bit.

'Um, he's still parking the car,' said Keith.

'This way?' said Aunty Bev, pushing the trolley on ahead.

They followed her, Keith's chest thumping with excitement.

'She's a bit of a gutful,' whispered Tracy, 'but I'm hoping your mum and dad'll knock her into shape.'

Keith decided not to say anything, not just yet.

Wouldn't be fair, telling a best mate who's still woozy from one of the world's most gruelling flights that she's got everything back to front.

*　　*　　*

'Nice car,' said Aunty Bev as they sped

along the motorway.

'Sixty-eight Jag,' said Dad. 'It's my boss's. He rebuilt it.'

'I think that's a wonderful thing to do,' said Aunty Bev, 'take old wrecks and restore them to their former glory.'

In the back Keith sighed happily.

He wondered if Dad knew she wasn't just talking about cars.

From the way Dad was grinning at her and nodding it looked like he did.

All I've got to do now, thought Keith, is make sure Dad and Mum don't start squabbling about which one of them Aunty Bev's going to fix up first.

He felt a tap on his arm.

'Brought you a prezzie,' said Tracy.

She was holding out a cane toad money box.

Keith took it, delighted.

'Thanks,' he said, 'it's just what I need.'

Trust a mate to know when your old money box was on its last legs.

Keith thanked Tracy again and asked her if she'd made it herself and she said she had and explained that the

70

hardest bit was getting its guts out through its bottom. Then Keith remembered he'd brought something for her. He pulled it out of his jeans pocket and unwrapped it.

'It's sausage and onion,' he said, 'to keep you going till we get home.'

'Ripper,' said Tracy, taking the sandwich eagerly. 'Thanks.'

'Tracy,' said Aunty Bev from the front, 'do you remember what we were yakking about on the plane? About how eating too much when you're sitting around a lot can give you a crook metabolism?'

Tracy paused with the sandwich halfway to her mouth.

Keith waited for her to tell Aunty Bev that those sort of theories didn't count for cane toad hunters with huge appetites.

Tracy sighed.

'Sorry,' she said. ' I forgot.'

She wrapped the sandwich up again.

Keith stared.

'It was a really nice thought,' she said to Keith. 'I'll have it later.'

Keith looked out the window,

stunned.

Must be the effect of the flight, he decided. Poor thing must be exhausted. Once she's had a chance to unpack and get her spine back to normal she'll be fine.

CHAPTER SEVEN

Keith sent an urgent message to Tracy.

Wake up.

Please.

The bedroom door stayed shut.

Come on, pleaded Keith silently, you've been in there for hours. Anyway, you shouldn't sleep too long directly after a long flight, you can get leg clots, it's a known fact.

The bedroom door stayed shut.

Tracy, continued Keith urgently, Mum'll be going to work in a sec.

'Keith, I'll be going to work in a sec,' called Mum from the bathroom.

Keith sighed.

Tragic.

A whole day of Mum being perked

up going to waste.

Well not if I can help it, he thought.

He headed for the bedroom door.

If he could get Tracy to cheer Mum up for just a couple of minutes now, Mum's posture would almost certainly improve a bit and male motorists were bound to notice while she was writing out their parking tickets.

'Keith,' called Mum, 'here a sec.'

Keith sighed and went into the bathroom.

Mum was brushing her hair in the mirror. Keith watched her sadly. On telly when women did that it made their hair thicker and bouncier. When Mum brushed hers it made it flatter.

'When Tracy and Bev wake up,' said Mum, 'make sure they have everything they want. The chocolate fingers are in the medicine cupboard.'

Keith looked at her.

She opened the bathroom cabinet and pointed to the top shelf.

Keith stood on tiptoe and could just see the chocolate-finger box.

Fair enough, he thought, they are a type of medicine.

'I put them up there so you wouldn't scoff them all,' said Mum.

Keith decided not to argue.

If he reminded her that she was the one with the chocolate-finger problem it would probably make her hair even flatter.

'Don't forget to clean your teeth,' he said to her, and hurried to the bedroom.

*   *   *

Tracy was stretched out on his bed asleep, still in her jeans and T-shirt.

Beside her on the pillow was the half-eaten sausage and onion sandwich.

He shook her gently.

She mumbled and turned over, still asleep.

'Tracy,' said Keith, 'it's urgent. I need you to tell Mum about your dad's cousin Phil.'

Tracy opened her eyes and stared at him blearily.

'Uh?' she mumbled.

'You know,' continued Keith, 'about how he got trampled in that rodeo, and

74

had to have thirteen metal pins surgically implanted in his body, which gave him good posture for the first time in his life plus greatly improved TV reception.'

Tracy rolled over.

'Not now,' she moaned into the pillow. 'I need more sleep. Aunty Bev didn't stop yakking the whole flight.'

Keith watched as her body went limp and her breathing became heavier.

Poor thing, he thought.

Normally she'd swim through wet cement to finish a sausage and onion sandwich and here she was, too tired to even pick out the fried onion.

'It'll only take a couple of minutes,' he said, 'then you can go back to sleep.'

She didn't stir.

Keith was debating whether to give her another shake when Mum appeared in the doorway.

'I'm going now love,' she said. 'Bye.'

'Mum, wait,' said Keith.

'What is it love?' she said.

Tracy started snoring.

'Doesn't matter,' said Keith.

Mum went.

Keith sighed, picked up the sandwich and took a bite.

Oh well, he thought, one more day won't kill her.

He opened his wardrobe and pulled out a blanket. While he was spreading it over Tracy he noticed something.

She was wearing the jeans she'd ripped crawling under a cane harvester to rescue a frightened blue-tongued lizard.

He saw how short they were on her now.

That day in the cane field they'd fitted her perfectly. She'd tucked them into her socks so snakes wouldn't crawl up her legs.

Now, only four months later, they stopped halfway down her ankles.

Keith stared.

Blimey, he thought. Swollen spinal fluid couldn't make that much difference. Either she's grown or those jeans have shrunk.

He glanced down at his own jeans and saw he was wearing the pair he'd ripped that day.

Just like old times.

Except his were still a perfect fit.

Which, come to think of it, was a bit strange.

He tried to think how his jeans could have got stretched. A power surge at the laundromat? Mum hanging them to dry over the bath with marbles in the pockets?

Then another possibility hit him.

*   *   *

Keith stared into Mum's bathroom mirror.

As usual all he could see was the top two-thirds of his face.

As usual the bottom of the mirror chopped him off under his nose like a badly-framed photograph.

Just like it had the first time he'd stood in front of it, three months ago.

He remembered how on that occasion he'd decided the previous tenant must have been a giant, or a circus artiste who liked to wear his stilts around the flat, and that was why the bathroom cabinet was so high on the wall.

The thought had made him smile, which had made him look strange in the mirror because he hadn't been able to see his mouth, just his twinkling eyes.

He still couldn't see his mouth.

Not even a bit of it.

Not even three months later.

And his eyes weren't twinkling at all now.

*   *   *

Keith burst into his bedroom at Dad's and gasped air into his aching lungs.

He'd never run non-stop from Mum's before.

But then he'd never had anything this urgent to double-check before.

Still panting, he went over to the boxes of tinned pineapple stacked beside the wardrobe.

Here goes, he thought.

He stood with his back against the boxes and ran the palm of his hand over the top of his head.

It was as he'd feared.

He was exactly the same height as

the stack.

He turned desperately and counted the boxes.

The stack was still only four boxes high.

Exactly as he and Dad had made it three months ago, because Dad had reckoned a kid shouldn't have piles of tinned pineapple in his room that were taller than he was, partly because of the danger of them falling on him and partly because of the scary shadows big stacks throw at night.

Keith felt more scared now than he ever had from tinned pineapple shadows.

Because this confirms it, he thought, heart pounding.

I've stopped growing.

*   *   *

'Aunty Bev, wake up.'

Keith tried the door again but it was definitely locked.

He wondered if Mum would mind him forcing her bedroom door open with the bread knife seeing as this was an emergency.

Before he could decide, he heard Aunty Bev moving around inside the room.

'Hang on,' she called.

Keith heard what sounded like the rustle of tissue boxes and the hiss of spray cans and the click of plastic lids.

Then Aunty Bev opened the door.

'G'day Keith,' she smiled.

Even though Keith was nearly frantic, he couldn't help gawking.

He'd never seen anyone who'd just been asleep for five hours in such good shape.

Her hair wasn't sticking out.

There were no pillow creases in her face.

He couldn't even see any dried dribble at the corners of her mouth.

Perhaps beauticians are trained to sleep sitting up, he thought, like camels.

'Anything the matter?' asked Aunty Bev.

Keith hesitated for a moment.

He felt a flash of embarrassment at the thought of blurting out his problem to someone he'd only met twice.

It's OK, he told himself. She's a professional. It's like going to the doctor.

'What can stop a person growing?' he asked. 'A person my age?'

Aunty Bev looked at him and frowned.

Keith hoped she wouldn't want to examine him physically.

'Hormones,' she said. 'If they're out of balance they can play havoc with your growth patterns.'

Keith knew that couldn't be it because he didn't have any hormones yet. Hormones made your voice go funny like Dennis Baldwin's, and his voice was still normal.

'What else?' he asked.

'Food,' said Aunty Bev. 'The more food you have the bigger you get. If you stop eating, you stop growing.'

Can't be that, thought Keith. I get heaps of food with Dad being in the business. Plus I'm pretty sure most of the major food groups are present in chocolate fingers.

'Anything else?' he asked.

Aunty Bev frowned again.

Keith hoped she wasn't going to say too much exercise. Not with the amount of running he was having to do between Mum and Dad's places.

'Stress,' she said. 'Tension, worry, anxiety, it can all give you a crook metabolism.'

Something clicked in Keith's brain.

'You mean,' he said, 'the sort of worry you feel when your parents have let themselves go so badly nobody wants to ask them out?'

Aunty Bev gently led him over to the settee.

'Keith,' she said, 'is there something you want to tell me?'

*   *   *

Keith was still glowing with happiness when he got to Dad's place, even though he felt a bit sick from drinking so much carrot juice.

Every time he thought about his chat with Aunty Bev, he glowed even more.

She'd been great.

'No problem,' she'd said after he'd

told her about Mum and Dad. 'You won't recognize them soon! She'd patted herself on the chest. 'Not now they've got their own personal grooming and fashion adviser. So you can stop worrying and go back to growing.'

Then, before she'd gone back to sleep, she'd told Keith how vegetable juice was full of growth vitamins and didn't make you fat, which was really good of her because he hadn't even asked.

'Hello, Keith.'

Dad was in the kitchen, putting instant coffee into a mug.

'Hello, Dad,' said Keith.

If he hadn't been so happy he'd have sighed.

Nine-thirty and Dad was already in his pyjamas.

Keith hoped that when Aunty Bev finished advising Dad on personal grooming and fashion and Dad started going to nightclubs, he'd remember to change out of his pyjamas first.

'What's that on your fingers?' asked Dad.

83

Keith saw that the fingers of his right hand were stained orange.

'Carrots,' he said. 'They were the only vegetables Mum had. I grated them for juice. It took three hours.'

'As long as it's not nicotine from cigarettes,' said Dad. 'Smoking'll stunt your growth and you wouldn't want that, would you?'

'No, Dad,' said Keith wearily.

He watched Dad fill the coffee mug from the hot tap and slouch back to the telly.

Keith sighed.

All the personal grooming and fashion advice in the world wouldn't be any use unless Dad perked up first.

OK Tracy, thought Keith, it's up to you.

CHAPTER EIGHT

Tracy stood next to Mum's fridge, eyes shining.

'A whole kitchen, seventeen storeys above the ground,' she breathed.

'Unreal.'

She went over to the sink and gazed out the window.

'There's another twenty-one kitchens above this one,' said Keith.

'Can we go up to the top floor?' said Tracy excitedly. 'It'll be really good practice for when I go to Nepal.'

'Nepal?' said Keith.

He wondered if he'd heard her right. Foreign words could be a bit hard to understand sometimes, especially if the person saying them had a mouthful of egg, sausage, bacon and onion sandwich.

Tracy swallowed and took another big mouthful.

'You must know Nepal,' she said. 'It's between India and Tibet.'

Keith remembered Tracy's travel brochure collection at her place in Australia, and how in the Campsites With Views bundle Nepal had even more brochures than New Zealand.

'Highest mountains in the world,' said Tracy wistfully, wiping her mouth on the back of her hand. 'It's gunna be great. They've got mountains there so high you need oxygen to get to the top. You dream about that when you come from a place that's three metres above sea level.'

Keith grinned.

He remembered how Tracy had climbed on to the roof of the post office in Orchid Cove to see if she could see Brisbane.

Then a thought hit him and he stopped grinning.

'When are you going?' he asked anxiously. 'You are still here for ten more days, aren't you?'

Tracy grinned.

'Course I am, you dope. I wouldn't come all this way and only stay for the weekend. We've got a stopover in Nepal on the way back.'

Keith felt weak with relief.

To do what he was about to ask her to do she'd need every one of those ten days, evenings included.

And she'd need all her strength.

'More to eat?' he asked.

'No thanks,' she said. 'I don't want to guzzle all your mum's food.'

'We've got tons,' he said. 'Do you

feel like some sugar cane?'

Before she could answer, Aunty Bev came into the kitchen.

Keith realized he was staring.

He didn't mean to but he'd never seen anyone wearing a tracksuit that tight before.

It was like she'd been sprayed with bright green paint.

He looked away in case she thought he was staring at her personal bits.

Which he had been.

I knew it, he said silently, but triumphantly. I knew it was possible for an adult to have a body without a single sag, droop or wobble.

'Mum's on early shift,' he said to her. 'Would you like some boiled peanuts?'

'Thanks mate,' said Aunty Bev, 'but I don't eat breakfast.'

Keith was amazed.

'Don't you get faint around eleven and start feeling sick?' he asked.

He realized Aunty Bev hadn't heard him.

She was looking at Tracy, who was licking the crumbs off her sandwich plate.

Without taking her eyes off Tracy, Aunty Bev slowly lifted one bright green arm.

For a moment Keith thought she was going to hit Tracy.

Then he saw she wasn't looking cross, just a bit exasperated.

He watched, puzzled, as Aunty Bev held her arm out in front of Tracy and pinched the underneath of it several times.

She did the same with the other arm.

Then she lifted one leg and tweaked underneath her thigh.

Blimey, thought Keith, she must be teaching Tracy aerobics.

Aunty Bev gave the underneath of her other thigh a couple of big tweaks, sighed long-sufferingly at Tracy and went into the living room.

Tracy rolled her eyes and scowled.

Grown-ups, thought Keith. When they decide to teach you something they never let up. It was the same with Dad and washing-up.

He rolled his eyes at Tracy in sympathy.

He decided not to say anything to

her about the aerobics. No point in upsetting her more. Plus, it might turn out to be yoga and he'd look like a wally.

Besides, he had more urgent things to talk to her about.

*   *   *

'Jeez.'

Tracy gazed up at the mural, her mouth open wide enough for a cane toad to hop in.

Two cane toads, thought Keith, if they didn't have much luggage.

'This leaves the mural at the new Orchid Cove baby health centre for dead,' said Tracy. 'Keith, you're a genius.'

Keith grinned and decided he'd done the right thing bringing Tracy here for their chat. Now she could see Mum and Dad's real selves and compare them to the poor broken-down creatures at home, she'd understand when he explained how urgently they needed perking up.

Tracy gripped his arm and looked at

him sympathetically.

Great, thought Keith, she's on the ball already.

'Hope the folks round here appreciate how much effort you put into cheering up their street,' said Tracy.

'Eh?' said Keith. 'Oh, yes, probably.'

He decided now was the time.

'Though actually,' he continued, 'I mostly did it for two folks in particular.'

'And we know who they are,' said a gloomy voice behind Keith, 'don't we?'

Keith spun round.

It was Mr Dodd, gazing up at the mural with a mournful expression.

'Gwen and Harvey Nottage in the travel agents, that's who,' he said. 'Sold more holidays in Spain since that thing went up than they have in the last five years. Just a pity it hasn't sold more of my paint.'

Keith sighed.

Bet the great painters of history didn't have to worry about sales figures, he thought.

He opened his mouth to remind Mr Dodd that most people who go on exotic, colourful holidays paint their houses when they get back, but Tracy spoke first.

'Course it won't sell paint,' she said to Mr Dodd, pointing up at the patches of bare brickwork in the top corners. 'It's not finished. To sell paint you need a full and even coverage.'

Mr Dodd stared up at the bare patches and scratched his head with his biro.

'You could be right,' he said, 'I hadn't thought of that.'

Good old Tracy, thought Keith. She tries to make everything OK even when she hasn't quite caught the drift.

'Thanks,' he whispered to Tracy, 'but I didn't do it just to sell paint. I did it to save . . .'

He realized Tracy couldn't hear him because she was too busy asking Mr Dodd if he had any rope.

*   *   *

'Blimey.'

Keith gazed up at Tracy as she lowered herself over the edge of

91

Mr Dodd's roof on the end of a nylon washing line.

Mr Dodd gripped Keith's shoulder in alarm.

'I thought she just wanted to tie the ladder to make it more secure,' croaked Mr Dodd.

Keith felt a bit croaky himself.

He stared up in amazement as Tracy hung off the rope by one hand, locked off the pulley above her head, took a brush from her back pocket, dipped it into the paint tin tied to her belt and dabbed Sky Blue on to a bare patch.

'Be careful,' he yelled.

'No worries,' shouted Tracy, 'I've been abseiling down Uncle Leo's grain silo since I was seven.'

Keith and Mr Dodd both gasped as Tracy swung across the mural, wrapped her legs round a downpipe and started brushing paint on to the other bare patch.

'Her uncle Leo must have nerves of steel,' croaked Mr Dodd.

'Plastic,' said Keith. 'He fell into a combine harvester and quite a lot of his body's been plastic since then.'

'So will quite a lot of your friend if she falls off that rope,' muttered Mr Dodd.

'She'll be OK,' said Keith.

If it was anyone else up there, he thought, I'd be sending them an urgent message not to fall off and get concussion and possibly brain damage.

But not Tracy.

She'll always be OK.

Suddenly he wanted to hug her for being the only person in his life he could rely on to be OK.

He still felt like hugging her when she'd hauled herself back on to the roof and climbed down into the shop, and handed the ropes and pulleys back to Mr Dodd and come outside to inspect the mural.

So he did.

She was startled at first, then hugged him back.

'Paint sales,' she said, rolling her eyes. 'Bet Picasso didn't have people whingeing at him about paint sales. Bet if he'd painted this, people'd be raving at him about the ripper colours on the houses and the way those weightlifters are so lifelike. How did you do that, it's great.'

Keith glowed.

'Actually,' he said, 'they're not weightlifters, they're Mum and Dad.'

Tracy stared at him.

'Your mum and dad?' she said.

'Yeah,' said Keith. 'Not the way they are now, the way they could be if someone perked them up and someone else helped them with fashion and personal grooming advice and they started going out on dates and rediscovered their real selves.'

Tracy stared up at Mum and Dad for a long time.

Then she turned to Keith.

'That's sick,' she said angrily.

Keith felt as if the mural, with the wall attached, had just fallen on him.

He tried to speak, but his brain felt like it was under 14 tons of bricks.

He watched as Tracy walked away down the street. He sent an urgent message to any part of his central nervous system that was listening.

Help.

Tracy stopped and walked back to

94

him, her face tight with anger.

'I don't know the way back,' she said.

Suddenly Keith knew what to do.

'This way,' he said.

He set off in the direction that would take them past Mr Mellish's.

*   *   *

'Bull.'

Tracy scowled at the gash on Mr Mellish's gatepost.

'It's true,' shouted Keith desperately. 'He died of loneliness and that's where they bashed into the gatepost with his body.'

'I don't mean that's bull,' said Tracy. 'What's bull is you trying to turn your mum and dad into Madonna and Tom Cruise just cos some poor old bloke died.'

Keith turned away so she wouldn't see his tears of frustration.

No point telling her I've stopped growing, he thought miserably. She'll say that's bull too.

Why was she carrying on like this?

Keith stared into the grey and murky

distance.

Tragic, he thought. A wonderful person like Tracy suffering from a mental condition brought on by her plane landing too quickly.

'I'm not trying to turn them into Madonna and Tom Cruise,' he said quietly, 'I'm just trying to save them and I need your help.'

'Perhaps they don't want to be saved,' said Tracy. 'Anyway, how do you know this old bloke died of loneliness?'

Keith took a deep breath.

'His ghost told me,' he said.

Before Tracy had a chance to laugh, Keith marched up to Mr Mellish's front door and pressed his ear to it.

In the distance, faint but unmistakable, he could hear the wailing.

'Listen for yourself,' he said to Tracy.

She hesitated, then came over and put her ear to the door.

'That's the neighbour's vacuum cleaner,' she said.

Keith closed his eyes.

He didn't care what she thought any more.

He concentrated on the mournful wailing.

'Don't give up,' it seemed to be saying. 'You've still got Aunty Bev.'

That's right, Keith thought, I have.

CHAPTER NINE

Keith looked at Dad standing at the stove in a cloud of smoke, bottom wobbling as he jiggled the frying pan.

He noted the damp strands of hair plastered across Dad's bald patch.

He took in the grease-stained Simpsons T-shirt that only just covered Dad's tummy bulge.

He stared at the baked bean sitting on Dad's left shoe.

He sighed with disappointment.

Come on Aunty Bev, thought Keith, you're meant to be Dad's personal grooming and fashion adviser. What have you been doing all day? You could at least have made a start on the ear hairs.

'Hello Keith,' said Dad. 'Where are the others?'

Keith explained that Aunty Bev and Tracy were coming over from Mum's shortly.

'You all right Keith?' asked Dad, concerned. 'You seem a bit in the dumps.'

'I'm OK,' said Keith, trying hard not to look like someone who'd spent part of the day being let down by his best friend, and the other part lying on his bed staring at the stack of tinned pineapple and trying to imagine what it'd be like going through life only four boxes high.

Being the only motorist in South London who couldn't reach the pedals of the car.

Being sent to bed early at business conferences.

Being pushed around by big pensioners at the club for the aged.

No point depressing Dad with all that.

Keith managed to give Dad half a smile.

Dad ruffled Keith's hair.

Suddenly Keith wanted to give himself a boot up the bum for being so self-centred.

What was being vertically challenged compared to being lonely and depressed and headed for an early grave?

Mum and Dad were the ones he should be worrying about.

'Righty-ho,' said Dad with a wink, 'well if you're feeling tip-top, perhaps you wouldn't mind whizzing Mr K's dinner over to him.'

He handed Keith a plate of liver and onions.

On his way over to Mr Kristos's table, Keith wondered why Dad sounded so cheerful.

For a fleeting moment he thought Tracy might have changed her mind and been round and perked Dad up.

Then he remembered Mum had said on the phone that Tracy and Aunty Bev had been at her place all afternoon.

Oh well, thought Keith, Len Tufnell must have been on time with the pork chops.

At least someone was trying to help.

Just as he reached Mr Kristos's table, Keith heard the door behind him swing open.

'G'day,' said Aunty Bev's voice. 'Sorry we're late.'

'Aha,' said Dad's voice, 'the guests of honour.'

Keith decided not to turn round.

He decided instead to have a long chat with Mr Kristos, and a long chat with each of the other customers, and with a bit of luck he wouldn't have to talk to Tracy all evening.

He might never have to talk to her again.

'G'day Keith,' said Tracy's voice softly.

Keith stopped in the middle of handing the plate to Mr Kristos.

He'd never heard Tracy so sad.

He turned round.

He'd never seen her so sad.

She stared at him, biting her lip.

He stared back helplessly, concern tugging at his insides.

'Do you want a piece of liver?' he said, holding out the plate.

'No thanks,' said Tracy quietly.

' 'Ere,' said Mr Kristos from his table, 'that's mine.'

While Keith handed over the liver to Mr Kristos, and Dad struggled to help Aunty Bev out of her skintight leather jacket, Keith's mind raced.

What had happened?

Had someone died?

Had Tracy's travel brochure collection been lost in a cyclone?

Why wasn't she saying anything?

Then he realized from her expression that she needed to talk to him in private.

* * *

On the way up the stairs Keith tried desperately to think what to say.

'Has your Dad's ligament gone septic and killed him?' seemed a bit blunt, especially if it had.

'If your travel brochures have been blown away in a cyclone I can get you some more from Mrs Nottage in the travel agents' sounded better.

But what if the cyclone had also

101

blown away something that couldn't be replaced? Like her parents or Buster the dog?

Keith still hadn't decided what to say by the time they got to his room.

Then he looked at Tracy's sad face again and the words just came out.

'What's up?' he said anxiously.

Tracy sighed.

'Aunty Bev's giving me a bit of a hard time, that's all,' she said. 'Carries on like a cracked record.'

Keith opened his mouth to say something about grown-ups who thought they were born aerobics or yoga or washing-up teachers, but before he could Tracy reached out and touched his arm.

'Keith,' she said, 'sorry I acted like a prawn this morning.'

Keith felt relief rush through him.

'That's OK,' he said, 'you were probably just a bit jet-lagged.'

Tracy thought about this and nodded.

'I can see you're really worried about your mum and dad,' she continued, 'and I'm gunna try and cheer them up.'

Keith felt like four boxes of tinned pineapple had been lifted from his shoulders.

He resisted the temptation to stick his head out of the window and yodel.

He didn't even give in the urge to do cartwheels round the room.

He just touched Tracy on the arm.

'Thanks,' he said.

He realized she wasn't listening.

'Jeez,' she said, 'do you get a bit hungry at night?'

*　　*　　*

Keith and Tracy walked back into the cafe.

They stopped and stared.

A tall, sophisticated figure was standing at the stove in a cloud of smoke jiggling a frying pan.

For a sec Keith thought Dad had gone off to watch telly and been replaced by a nightclub playboy in a tropical shirt who liked to cook his own sausages.

Then the figure stepped out of the smoke and Keith saw it was Dad.

'What do you think?' grinned Dad, modelling the shirt. 'Bit of all right, eh?'

Even the parrots on the shirt looked impressed with how smart they were.

Keith tingled with excitement.

'Yes,' he said, 'brilliant.'

'And,' said Dad, 'smell.'

He bent over and Keith sniffed his neck. A sweet, spicy aroma of tropical fruit and seaweed and air freshener filled Keith's nostrils.

'Barrier Reef For Men,' said Dad. 'The real stuff.'

Keith felt dizzy, partly from the amount of Barrier Reef Dad was wearing, and partly from happiness.

'Couple of little prezzies,' said Aunty Bev, 'to say thanks for your dad's hospitality.' She gave Keith a big wink.

Keith beamed at her and wondered if people who wore really tight clothes could be nominated as saints.

'OK,' said Dad, 'let's eat.'

He led them all over to the stove and Keith saw what was on the benchtop.

A bowl of creamy batter.

Pieces of cod in matzo flour.

Hand-cut potatoes.

'Fish and chips!' yelled Keith in delight.

Just like the old days.

It was working.

Dad really was perking up.

'Yum,' said Tracy, 'I'm starving.'

While Dad slid the fish through the batter and dropped them into a big pan of foaming oil, Keith glanced around the cafe.

The customers were taking notice of the new Dad too.

A couple of women over by the window couldn't take their eyes off him, and they were both over seventy.

*   *   *

As Keith and Tracy and Aunty Bev and Dad ate the fish and chips, Keith decided it was the best meal he'd had since Mum and Dad split up.

Even though Aunty Bev only ate three mouthfuls of fish and no chips.

'Would you prefer sausages?' Keith asked her. 'Or a burger?'

Aunty Bev just smiled and shook her

head.

What a trooper, thought Keith. Doesn't want to offend Dad.

Then Tracy told them about her second cousin Glennys who made fish sausages once and nearly choked the cat because she forgot to take the bones out.

Dad chuckled.

Aunty Bev added that she wasn't surprised as Glennys always ate prawns with the shells on.

Dad roared.

It continued to be Keith's best meal right up to the point where Dad offered Tracy seconds.

'Yes please,' said Tracy, 'this fish is tops.'

Before Dad could put a couple more pieces on Tracy's plate, Aunty Bev raised an arm.

Keith sent her an urgent message.

Leave it out.

The message didn't get through.

Aunty Bev began tweaking.

Tracy's face fell.

'Actually,' she said, 'I won't have any more, thanks.'

106

'Are you sure?' said Dad.

'I'm feeling a bit tired,' said Tracy. 'I think I'll go and lie down for a bit.'

Keith watched her go with concern.

'Is she OK?' said Dad.

'Just a bit highly-strung,' said Aunty Bev. 'Always has been.'

Funny, thought Keith, I've never noticed that.

He resisted the temptation to tell Aunty Bev how too much aerobics could be damaging for kids whose bones were still growing.

After all, Aunty Bev was almost a saint.

But as soon as he'd eaten Tracy's bits of fish, he went up to see how she was.

*   *   *

The first thing Keith saw as he got to the top of the stairs were the tins lying on his bedroom floor.

Corned beef.

Apricot halves.

Both empty.

Then, as he reached the doorway, he saw Tracy.

She was sitting on his bed reading one of his video-game magazines and spooning baked beans into her mouth with the fold-out spoon on her Swiss Army knife.

Poor thing, thought Keith. Her body clock's all haywire. One minute she wants to go to bed, the next she wants to have breakfast.

'Tracy,' he said softly, 'why don't you ask Aunty Bev to leave the aerobics till you've got over your jet lag? She's a reasonable woman, she'll understand.'

Tracy stared at him, startled.

He waited for her to say something.

She tried to, but Keith could see she couldn't find the right words.

He was glad he hadn't had jet lag this bad when he went to Australia.

Suddenly Tracy jumped up and dropped the tin and pushed past him and ran down the stairs.

Keith stood there for a second, stunned, watching the baked beans make a puddle on the floor.

Then he realized what was going on.

'Wait,' he shouted as he hurried down after her. 'It's OK. They're for you.'

CHAPTER TEN

Sometimes, thought Keith, as his feet pounded the dark pavement and his lungs burned, it can be a real pain having a best friend who can run faster than you.

He didn't catch up with Tracy till they were almost at Mum's block of flats.

She was standing under a street light looking lost and tearful.

'It's OK,' he gasped, collapsing against the light pole, 'you can eat as much of that stuff as you like. Mr Kristos doesn't mind.'

She didn't seem to hear.

She was glaring up at the tower blocks looming all around them.

'I've forgotten which one's your mum's,' she said angrily, wiping her eyes on the back of her hand. 'Pretty dumb, eh?'

Keith was shocked.

Tracy's sense of direction was legendary in Orchid Cove. Mr

Gambaso in the milk bar reckoned you could blindfold her anywhere in North Queensland and she'd find her way to his hamburger counter without help.

'Come on,' said Keith gently, 'this way.'

On the way over to Mum's block Keith composed a letter to the airlines suggesting they put a notice in their inflight magazines warning that jet lag could play greater havoc with people's bedtimes and sense of direction than was generally believed.

As they climbed the stairs to Mum's floor, Keith took Tracy's hand to show her he understood.

After a few seconds she pulled her hand away.

'I'm all right,' she said quietly.

While he let her into the flat, he tried to think of something else he could do to help.

'Would you like a sandwich?' he asked. 'I've got some Vegemite and tinned beetroot.'

'No thanks,' she said. 'I just want to go to bed.'

She went into the bedroom and

closed the door.

Keith sighed.

Poor old Tracy, he thought. She's probably homesick as well.

He decided to make the Vegemite and beetroot sandwich anyway. Even if she didn't feel like eating it, just looking at it would probably make her feel better.

He was on his way to the kitchen when someone came out of the bathroom.

Keith blinked.

For a fleeting second he thought they were being burgled by someone with attractive hair and good posture.

Then he realized it was Mum.

She was wearing a lilac tracksuit that hugged her body.

Her hair was curly and bounced as she walked.

Her face was smooth and her eyelashes were thick and her lips were red.

Keith knew, heart pounding with excitement, that it wasn't because she'd been eating beetroot sandwiches.

'Mum,' he said, 'you look great.'

'Bev needed a guinea pig to try out some new beauty products on,' she said with an embarrassed grin. 'And to say thank you she insisted I borrow this outfit. I can only just squeeze into it.'

Keith could see what she meant.

Think positive, he told himself. It's meant to be skintight. Mum's just got a bit more skin than Aunty Bev, that's all. At least she's holding her tummy in and keeping her shoulders back.

'It's a knockout,' he said happily.

'I'm glad you're home early,' said Mum. 'I was about to ring you at the cafe to let you know I've just been invited away for the weekend.'

Keith stared at her in delight.

'It's only for two nights,' she said quickly, 'with some people from work. They've got a caravan at Bognor.'

Keith wanted to throw his arms round her and give her a hug, but was afraid she'd smudge.

You're a wonder Aunty Bev, he thought joyfully, a blinking marvel.

It was working.

Everything was going to be OK.

'They're picking me up in half an

hour,' said Mum. 'I know it's very short notice, what with Tracy and Bev being here . . .'

'Mum,' said Keith, struggling to keep his voice from wobbling, 'I want you to go.'

*　　　*　　　*

Keith crept into the bedroom.

As his eyes got used to the gloom he saw Tracy lying on the bed, eyes closed.

Carefully he put the Vegemite and beetroot sandwich on the chest of drawers next to her.

He sent her a quiet message.

When you wake up, I hope the jet lag's gone and I hope seeing something familiar makes being in a strange country a bit less stressful.

Tracy opened her eyes.

'Keith,' she said, 'I reckon what you're doing to your mum and dad sucks.'

Keith opened his mouth but nothing came out.

'You're trying to make them into something they're not,' she said, 'and I

113

reckon that's crook.'

Keith tried to stay calm.

She can't help it, he reminded himself, she's just having a relapse.

It was no good.

He felt his face getting hot.

'I'm trying to save them from being alone,' he said.

Tracy sat up.

'Perhaps they want to be alone,' she said.

Sometimes, thought Keith with an exasperated sigh, best mates can be really thick.

'Nobody wants to be alone,' he said. 'Look at Mr Mellish. Being alone killed him.'

'How do you know?' said Tracy.

Keith decided that all long-distance planes should have a health warning printed on them.

FLYING CAN INJURE YOUR BRAIN.

'Because,' said Keith, 'he told me. And he told me it could happen to Mum and Dad. He came back from the dead to tell me.'

Tracy swung her legs off the bed and

pulled her shoes on.

'Prove it,' she said.

*   *   *

Keith crouched by Mr Mellish's back steps, his heart thumping, partly from the sprint across the garden, partly because he was worried the neighbours had heard and were at that moment rummaging around for torches and kitchen knives, but mostly because he couldn't hear a single mournful wail.

He strained his ears.

Nothing.

'Well,' said Tracy, 'what now?'

Keith thought frantically.

He needed something to keep her occupied while he tried to make contact with Mr Mellish.

Keith turned to her dark shape crouched next to him.

'See if you can find a key,' he whispered. 'Mind out for glass, I broke a milk bottle last time.'

While Tracy shone her torch around the steps, Keith sent an urgent message to Mr Mellish.

Sorry about this, I know it's rude disturbing you this late, but if you could explain the situation to Tracy it would be a huge help. Thanks.

He strained his ears again.

There it was.

Very faint.

Almost drowned out by the distant hum of traffic.

But definitely a wail.

'Ow!' said Tracy.

'Shhh,' whispered Keith, 'I can hear him.'

'I've just cut myself,' said Tracy.

Keith sighed.

It was his fault for allowing a jet-lagged person near broken glass.

'But I've found the key,' she whispered. 'It must have been in the milk bottle.'

Keith took the torch and had a look at the cut. It was on one of Tracy's fingers and even though it was small it was bleeding quite a lot.

Keith offered her his hanky, but she said no.

He turned his attention back to listening.

The wail was still there.

Just.

'Hear it?' he whispered.

'No,' said Tracy.

'Don't suck so loud,' said Keith.

Tracy stopped sucking her finger and listened.

'I still can't hear it,' she said.

Keith took a deep breath and licked his dry lips.

He hoped they wouldn't have to do this, but now he realized they had no choice.

'Come on,' he whispered, his heart thumping even louder than before, 'you'll hear better inside.'

*   *   *

Inside the dark house Keith sent an urgent message to the fish and chips in his stomach.

Don't panic.

Stay where you are.

This is just the normal musty smell of a house that's been shut up for a bit.

It is not, repeat not, the smell of rotting flesh hanging off the putrid and decomposing body of a ghost.

'I still can't hear anything,' said Tracy.

Keith listened.

She was right.

The wailing had stopped.

'He's probably just having a rest,' whispered Keith. 'You probably get out of breath easily when you're dead.'

Tracy took the torch and shone it around.

A ghostly white shape loomed over them.

Keith flinched.

But it wasn't Mr Mellish, it was the water heater above the kitchen sink.

'Look,' whispered Keith as the torchlight shone on a pile of mould-covered plates. 'Vegetable scraps. Meat scraps. Bread scraps. He obviously didn't die of a bad diet.'

Keith took the torch and shone it into the cupboards.

'No empty bottles,' he added, 'so it couldn't have been drink.'

He shone the torch around the kitchen.

'And no microwave,' he concluded,

'so it wasn't a radiation leak.'

He shone the torch on Tracy.

'Looks like it was loneliness all right,' he said sadly.

'Or his heart going bung,' said Tracy. 'Or cancer. Or him choking on a veggie. Or . . .'

Tracy stopped.

She listened intently.

Keith could hear it too.

The mournful wail.

'See,' whispered Keith, heart pounding, 'he's telling us it was loneliness and we've got to save Mum and Dad from the same fate. Satisfied? OK, let's go home now.'

He tried to steer Tracy towards the back door, but she took the torch and pulled away from him.

'Let's have a squiz,' she said and moved off into the darkness towards the wail.

'Wait,' said Keith, following her down a narrow hallway, 'he might not want to meet us in person.'

A stairway loomed up to his left.

'It's coming from upstairs,' said Tracy. 'Come on.'

Keith felt sick.

Nice one, he thought as he went after her up the stairs, forty million best mates in the world and I get the maniac cane-toad hunter with the guts of steel.

Still, he told himself as they crept along the landing towards the open door, the wail was coming through, that's probably just as well. Because when we see what's in that bedroom I've only got fish and chips to keep down, but she's got corned beef, apricot halves and baked beans.

As they slowly poked their heads round the door, Tracy gripped his arm.

She was shaking just as much as him.

He hoped that when they'd finished screaming she wouldn't be too exhausted to run for it.

The torch lit up the room.

Keith opened his mouth to yell.

But he didn't.

Because in the neat little bedroom with its neat little bed there wasn't a ghost to be seen.

Just a small, thin, shivering, wailing black and grey dog.

CHAPTER ELEVEN

Keith and Tracy and the dog were all still shivering when they got back to Mum's place.

'Hope it hasn't caught a chill in the night air,' said Keith, anxiously peeking inside his jacket for signs of a runny nose.

The dog peered out at him with mournful eyes.

Keith could feel its ribs quivering against his own.

'Dogs are pretty tough,' said Tracy. 'Buster shut himself in the freezer once and we didn't find him for twenty minutes. Would have been longer except we heard him coughing up frozen peas.'

Keith stroked the dog's head.

'You're probably right,' he said. 'It's probably just suffering from overexcitement like us.'

'That and not having anything to eat or drink for nine days,' said Tracy.

They all had some warm milk, and

then the dog had some more.

And some more.

And some more.

By the time it had finished its fourth bowl they'd all stopped shivering.

Keith and Tracy lay on the kitchen floor watching the dog lick milk off its paws and face.

'Amazing,' said Keith. 'I couldn't go nine hours without food, let alone nine days.'

'Wolves can go ages without food,' said Tracy, 'and all dogs are descended from wolves. Except Buster, he's descended from a garbage disposal unit.'

The dog was looking at Keith again with its sad eyes.

'Shouldn't we give it some solids?' said Keith.

'Not too much at first,' said Tracy, 'or it'll get gut-ache. Try it with a bit of sugar cane.'

Keith got the sugar cane out of the fridge and sawed a piece off with the bread knife and put it on the floor in front of the dog.

The dog sniffed it, chewed it halfheartedly, then went to sleep.

'Buster does the same thing with cane toads,' said Tracy.

Keith lifted the dog on to his jacket and watched its ribs rise and fall under its straggly black and grey fur.

'Poor thing,' said Keith. 'Do you think it knows Mr Mellish is dead?'

Tracy shook her head. 'That's why it stayed by the bed. Waiting for him to come back.'

Keith's eyes suddenly felt prickly.

He swallowed and took a deep breath.

'I'll have a chat with it,' he said, 'when it's got its strength back.'

'Wonder why the ambulance officers and the police left it behind?' said Tracy.

'Must have thought there'd be relatives coming round to collect it and do the washing up,' said Keith. 'Mustn't have known Mr Mellish's death was such a tragically lonely one.'

'Keith,' said Tracy quietly, 'don't be a dope. How could Mr Mellish die of loneliness when he had such a loyal and devoted friend in the house?'

Later, curled up in Mum's bed on the settee, Keith finally worked it out.

OK, he thought, so Mr Mellish didn't die of loneliness.

But that was only because he had a dog to love him and keep him company and perk him up.

Mum and Dad haven't got that.

All they've got is me and Tracy and Aunty Bev.

They're depending on us.

Keith looked at the dog breathing quietly next to him.

He felt very fond of it already.

You brave little thing, he thought. You'd have starved to death worrying about your master.

Bit like me, stunting my growth worrying about Mum and Dad.

He gave the dog a hug.

Except I'm lucky, he thought. Thanks to me worrying, Mum and Dad are going to be OK.

* * *

'Dazzle?' said Tracy, exploding with laughter and spraying cereal across the kitchen. 'You've called him Dazzle?'

'Yes,' said Keith, giving Dazzle a third helping of Irish stew. 'I like it. And we don't know what his real name is.'

'I doubt if it's Dazzle,' said Tracy. 'Pretty unusual name, but.'

'I got the idea from something Aunty Bev once said,' replied Keith. 'Dazzle the punters.'

'I should have guessed,' said Tracy bitterly. 'That's the sort of thing that prawn-brain would say.'

Keith stared at her, stunned.

'Keep your voice down,' he stammered, 'she'll hear you.'

'She went out early,' said Tracy. 'Gone to make your dad look even more dopey.'

Keith felt anger rush through him.

'Aunty Bev,' he said, 'is saving the lives of two seriously depressed people. And that's more important than whether she nags a bit about aerobics.'

Tracy frowned for a moment, then

wearily put her cereal spoon down and looked hard at Keith.

'Aunty Bev,' she said, 'is a fanatic. If she came in here now and saw Dazzle stuffing his face with Irish stew, do you know what she'd say?'

'What?' asked Keith, wondering if a person could get inflammation of the brain from cutting their finger on a dirty milk bottle.

'She'd say,' mimicked Tracy angrily, ' "Dazzle, mate, that extra helping'll go straight to your thighs and hips, and then you'll be dumpy and no one'll like you and everyone'll laugh at you and you'll be lonely and unhappy for the rest of your life".'

Keith stared at her.

'How do you know?' he asked.

'Because,' said Tracy tearfully, standing up and tweaking underneath her arms, 'that's what she says to me.'

*   *   *

Tragic, thought Keith as he left Mum's block.

His ears were still ringing from Tracy

slamming the bedroom door in his face.

All he'd done was try and talk a bit of sense to her.

Suggest to her that Aunty Bev was probably just worried about her because she'd grown upwards so fast it could mean her metabolism was a bit unstable and she was in danger of growing outwards very fast too.

She hadn't even let him finish.

Slam.

'I'm worried about her too,' Keith said to Dazzle. 'I think this might be something more than jet lag.'

Dazzle nodded.

He understands me, thought Keith.

Either that or he's not used to having string tied to his collar.

'G'day Keith,' said a cheery voice.

Keith looked up.

Aunty Bev was striding towards him in her pink tracksuit.

'Didn't know you had a dog,' she said. She stopped and patted Dazzle. 'He's in lovely condition, but. Not an ounce of fat on him.'

'Aunty Bev,' said Keith, 'did you and

Tracy have any injections to stop you getting typhoid and cholera when you go to Nepal?'

'Yes,' she said, 'why?'

'I'm worried about Tracy,' he replied. 'I think she might be allergic to them.'

'Is she sick?' asked Aunty Bev, concerned.

'No,' said Keith, 'just sort of emotional.'

Aunty Bev nodded.

'I'll go and have a chat with her,' she said. 'No drama. Her hormones are playing up a bit at the moment, that's all.'

Keith felt relief trickle through him.

Hormones.

Of course.

'Go and say g'day to your dad,' grinned Aunty Bev. 'That's if you recognize him.'

Keith watched Aunty Bev hurry into the flats.

'That woman,' he said to Dazzle, 'is a saint.'

Dazzle did a pee on the pavement.

                    *   *   *

On the way to the cafe Keith decided it
would either be a new suit or a wig.

He imagined Dad's bald patch
covered with thick luxurious hair.

He grinned.

Nice one.

Then a thought hit him.

Wigs had to be made to measure.
Even Aunty Bev couldn't get a wig
made on a Saturday morning.

'Unless,' he said to Dazzle, who was
panting inside Keith's jacket trying to
lick his face, 'they got lucky and picked
up one his size second-hand from the
classifieds.'

He pushed open the cafe door and
went in.

'Hello Keith,' said Dad, looking up
from the table he was wiping. He ran
his hand over his head. 'What do you
think?'

Oh no, thought Keith.

Please no.

He stared in horror.

CHAPTER TWELVE

It was the worst haircut Keith had ever seen.

'Bev reckons short hair looks better on balding men,' said Dad. 'She's right, eh?'

Keith sighed.

The longest hairs on Dad's entire head were the ones growing out of his ears.

Keith sent an urgent message to his own head.

Be positive.

Nod.

But it wouldn't.

'You'll use much less shampoo,' said Keith after a bit.

It was the best he could do.

Dad grinned and moved on to the next table.

Keith sent Dad's hair an urgent message.

Grow back.

Please.

Later in the weekend Keith saw another haircut just as bad.

The same bristles all over the scalp.

The same sticking-out veins on the temples.

Even the same hair in the ears.

Keith stared at it.

Oh well, he thought, at least Dad's not the only one.

But he didn't feel any better.

It was hard to when the only other haircut in London as tragic as Dad's belonged to an escaped convict who'd killed eight people with a whale knife.

Keith reached up and ran his fingers over the murderer's bristles.

They felt exactly the same as Dad's.

'Hey you,' said a museum attendant, 'no touching the exhibits.'

'Sorry,' said Keith.

He pointed at the wax figure of the murderer.

'Would you invite someone who looks like him to the pictures,' he asked the attendant, 'if you knew he was kind and gentle and a whiz with fried

131

foods?'

The attendant smiled.

'Only if I was his mother,' she said.

Keith sighed and went back over to Dad and Aunty Bev.

'Glad you came?' Aunty Bev was saying to Dad.

'You can say that again,' said Dad. 'Best wax museum in Britain and it took a foreigner to bring me here.'

Aunty Bev grinned and pretended to clout him round the head with her bag.

Dad pretended to duck.

Keith noticed a small roll of fat appear at the top of Dad's neck.

It'll take weeks for the hair to grow back over that, thought Keith gloomily.

Months probably.

'A manicurist at a beauty therapy conference in Townsville told me about this place,' said Aunty Bev. She pointed to a nineteenth-century fish shop assistant who minced up her neighbour's children. 'Look at those exquisite nails.'

Dad leaned forward to look and his bottom wobbled.

Keith sighed again.

He looked at the flat stomach and firm buttocks of the police officer who was arresting the fish shop assistant, and wished you could get wax parents.

At least if they were beyond help you could melt them down and start again.

*   *   *

A bit later Dad lingered to look at a famous chef and Keith found himself walking on with Aunty Bev.

'Suits him, eh, the haircut?' she said, glancing back at Dad. 'Short hair always looks better on balding men.'

Keith didn't know what to say.

He wished he'd stayed at home with Tracy and Dazzle.

Then he told himself to stop being silly.

OK, he thought, Aunty Bev made a mistake with the haircut. That doesn't mean she's a prawn-brain. Even highly-skilled professionals make mistakes sometimes.

Keith looked back at Dad, who was studying the contents of the chef's saucepan with his hands in his pockets and his tummy bulging under the parrot shirt.

Think positive, Keith told himself. There's still heaps Aunty Bev can do.

'Aunty Bev,' he said, 'have you done much work with tummies and bottoms?'

'You mean sculpting the basic lines of the body,' said Aunty Bev.

Keith thought that was probably what he meant.

'Exercise and stuff,' he said.

He had a vision of Aunty Bev making Dad do push-ups with a box of tinned pineapple on his back.

He grinned.

If that didn't cure bottom wobble, nothing would.

'Exercise is OK,' said Aunty Bev, 'but it doesn't go far enough. I prefer a combination of diet and cosmetic surgery.'

'Cosmetic surgery?' said Keith. 'What's that?'

'It means when bits of your body are stopping you looking good, you have them altered or cut off,' said Aunty Bev. 'Bits of skin, flesh, even bone.'

134

Keith stared at her.

Cut off?

With a scalpel?

Just to look good?

Keith had a vision of Dad without his bottom.

He felt dizzy and a bit sick.

'I think liposuction would be perfect for your dad,' said Aunty Bev.

'Liposuction?' said Keith. 'What's that?'

He wasn't sure he wanted to know.

'It's very clever,' said Aunty Bev. 'They've got a special sort of vacuum cleaner that can suck the fat out from under your skin.'

Keith sat down next to an attendant and hoped he wouldn't be sick over her handbag.

'Of course that leaves the skin a bit baggy,' continued Aunty Bev, 'so they have to cut some strips out and seam it up. Like having jeans taken in.'

Keith realized what was going on.

Aunty Bev was sending him up.

Joking.

He glanced over to see if the attendant was getting it.

The attendant didn't seem to be.

The attendant was looking a bit queasy too.

'I've had it done,' said Aunty Bev, running her hand down her neck.

Keith looked at her.

She wasn't joking.

'It'll be time for Tracy to have it done in a couple of years,' she said.

Keith gaped.

Tracy?

He had another vision.

A wax Aunty Bev standing between the Whale Knife Killer and the Fish Shop Mincer holding a blood-stained vacuum cleaner.

*   *   *

On the way home, after Dad and Aunty Bev had said goodbye and gone off to the pictures, Keith told himself to calm down.

Aunty Bev wouldn't let Tracy have her fat vacuumed unless she really needed it.

Course she wouldn't.

Aunty Bev's a trained professional.

Look at the great job she's done with Mum.

*   *   *

'Keith,' called Mum's voice as he closed the front door, 'is that you?'

A pit opened up in Keith's stomach.

He recognized the tone in her voice.

It was the tone she'd used when she told him she and Dad were going to split up.

Oh no, thought Keith. Her weekend's been a disaster.

But how could it have been?

She'd looked wonderful.

Men would have been flocking to Bognor just for a look.

'Yes,' said Keith, 'it's me.'

What could have gone wrong?

Then Dazzle ran out of the kitchen and Keith realised what must have happened.

Mum must have come home, found Dazzle, plus a big puddle on the carpet, and now Mum was going to tell him that Dazzle had to go.

'Please let me keep him,' pleaded

Keith as Mum came out of the kitchen. 'He's been under a lot of emotional stress, but he'll start controlling his bladder soon, I promise, please.'

'Keith,' said Mum, 'it's OK. Tracy's explained about Dazzle. I don't mind you having him as long as you take responsibility for him and keep him off the beds.'

Keith's insides soared.

Then dropped again.

He stared at Mum.

Her hair was flat.

Her face was pale.

She was wearing her old baggy shorts.

Keith could see her leg veins even though the lighting was low.

He felt like giving her a shake.

'Mum,' he felt like yelling, 'how can you expect to meet people and fall in love and be happy if you won't leave your make-up and your lilac tracksuit on?'

He didn't, because while he was thinking about it a man followed Mum out of the kitchen.

'This is Donald,' said Mum.

138

The man took Mum's hand.

'Hello Keith,' he said. 'I've heard lots about you.'

Keith opened his mouth, but it felt like it was made of wax.

'Donald and me work together,' said Mum quietly. 'And we're going out together as well.'

Keith saw she didn't just mean tonight.

Suddenly his mouth was working.

'Did you meet this weekend?' he asked.

Mum and Donald exchanged a look.

'No,' said Mum in a small voice. 'We've been going out for about six weeks.'

Keith's whole head felt like it was made of wax.

Six weeks.

'Just at lunchtimes and after work,' said Mum. 'I didn't want to tell you until I knew it was serious. I'm sorry love, I know this must be a shock for you.'

Keith lowered his eyes.

Just above Mum's ankle, he saw, was a leg vein in the shape of a mouth laughing at him.

CHAPTER THIRTEEN

Keith gazed at half of London spread out shimmering below him and felt the sun on his cheeks and the breeze in his hair and tried not to think about how many people down there were having their fat vacuumed.

Think positive.

It's a knockout summer day, he told himself, and I'm having a picnic with my best friend and the view's brilliant and I've got a really nice dog and Mum's had the incredible good fortune to find the one man in London who doesn't mind road-map legs and Dad's pulling himself together very nicely thank-you, and will almost certainly be swept off his feet by crowds of women just as soon as his hair grows a bit.

Keith felt his guts relax.

It was working.

He was feeling happy.

Now all he had to do was cheer

Tracy up.

He took a big breath.

'Mmmm,' he said to Tracy, 'the air's so fresh up here. Hardly any pong from the chemical works. It's giving me an appetite.'

Tracy didn't reply.

'I love picnics out of tins,' said Keith, 'don't you?'

Tracy didn't reply.

Keith spooned cold Irish stew into his mouth and poured the rest into Dazzle's bowl and watched the cars far below glinting in the sunlight.

'Great view, eh?' he said to Tracy. 'I bet even people from Nepal would be impressed by this view.'

Tracy didn't reply.

Keith saw she'd flopped down on Mum's tablecloth among the tins and was staring at the sky.

She still hadn't eaten anything.

Not the apricot halves or the spaghetti or the peas or the Irish stew or the fruit salad in heavy syrup.

Keith sighed.

She looked so miserable.

'Of course,' he said, 'they probably

don't have thirty-eight-storey blocks of flats in Nepal, not ones with flat roofs that are good for picnics. But the mountains sound great. I bet the views from them are brilliant.'

Tracy didn't reply.

Dazzle finished the Irish stew and went over and licked her cheek.

She didn't even seem to notice that.

Keith sighed again.

It wasn't working.

Him being happy wasn't making her feel better.

He took another deep breath and tried to think what else he could do.

'I know,' he said, 'let's go tenpin bowling.'

Tracy looked at him and shook her head.

Keith was shocked. It was the first time he'd ever seen her refuse an invitation to play a sport, including rugby league.

This is hopeless, he thought.

Before he could get back to thinking positive, a cry rang out.

'There you are!'

Aunty Bev emerged from the

stairwell and came across the roof towards them.

Keith groaned inside and Tracy groaned out loud.

'Your dad reckoned you'd probably be up here,' called Aunty Bev. 'Jeez, this view's even better than the one from the silo at Uncle Leo's.'

'Keith,' pleaded Tracy, 'make her go away.'

'Aunty Bev,' said Keith, 'Tracy's not feeling so hot at the moment, so I was going to let her have a bit of a snooze up here on her own. Do you like tenpin bowling?'

Aunty Bev didn't reply.

She was crouched down examining the empty tin of Irish stew.

'Sometimes Tracy,' she said wearily, 'I think you want to be a lardbucket.'

Keith was about to point out that many top athletes had large appetites, not to mention some of the world's best racehorses, when Tracy leapt to her feet.

'Leave me alone!' she screamed at Aunty Bev. 'Rack off and leave me alone!'

Keith watched horrified as Tracy ran across the roof and down into the stairwell.

He could feel Dazzle cowering behind his legs.

He turned to Aunty Bev.

'It wasn't Tracy,' he said. 'Me and Dazzle had it.'

Aunty Bev patted his arm.

'S'OK mate,' she said, 'I'm not crook at you. In fact I've been meaning to thank you for giving me the idea of coming over here with Tracy. Get her away from those parents of hers. They haven't got a clue what they've got with that kid. She could be a top international model one day if she wasn't such a guts.'

Keith stared at her.

Tracy, a model?

The girl who could haul herself on to a steep tin roof at night in a downpour and catch cane toads with a torch and a bucket and no bait?

What a waste.

Keith was about to tell Aunty Bev that she'd got Tracy all wrong, that she was trying to turn Tracy into a person Tracy wasn't, when something distracted him.

In each of the mirrored lenses in Aunty Bev's sunglasses Keith could see his own face staring back at him.

*   *   *

Tracy was huddled in a corner on the thirty-six floor landing.

Keith had never seen anyone crying so hard.

He went over, feeling in his pockets for a hanky.

He couldn't find one, so he put his arms round her.

'I can't stand much more of this,' sobbed Tracy. 'If she doesn't stop this I'm gunna end up like Dawn Rickson.'

'Who's Dawn Rickson?' asked Keith.

'Kid in my school,' said Tracy between ragged breaths. 'Thought she was fat. Stuck her fingers down her throat every day after lunch and made herself chuck. Even after they took her to hospital. Poor thing.'

Dazzle poked his head out of Keith's jacket and licked the tears on Tracy's cheeks.

'You won't have to do that,' said Keith quietly. 'Aunty Bev is going to stop because we're going to make her.'

Tracy didn't say anything.

Keith kept his arms round her.

After a while they heard Aunty Bev go down in the lift.

Quite a bit later Tracy gave a wobbly sigh.

'Hope you're right,' she whispered.

CHAPTER FOURTEEN

Keith found Aunty Bev at Dad's place, curled up on the settee reading a glossy magazine with a woman on the front even thinner than she was.

He cleared his throat until she looked up.

'I think what you're doing to Tracy is wrong,' he said, 'and I think you should stop.'

Aunty Bev looked at him for what seemed like months.

Keith's stomach felt like it was being

jabbed from the inside by a whole lot of chocolate fingers.

A muscle in his left buttock was quivering.

He wondered if his stomach was sagging and his bottom was wobbling.

Don't care if they are, he thought.

Then Aunty Bev smiled.

'You're a good mate to Tracy,' she said. 'Tracy's lucky to have you. But you don't know what you're talking about.'

'Yes I do,' said Keith softly.

Aunty Bev closed her magazine.

'Keith,' she said, 'I'm a beautician. I'm trained to know what's best for people.'

'Only on the outside,' said Keith.

Keith noticed that even though Aunty Bev's head was completely still, her plastic parrot earrings were trembling.

This is it, he thought. This is where she either agrees with me or attacks me with a vacuum cleaner.

Aunty Bev suddenly stood up.

Keith flinched, then remembered Dad's Hoover was broken.

'You probably think Tracy's just got a bit of puppy fat, right?' said Aunty Bev. 'You probably think all kids put on a bit of weight at your age and it's perfectly OK.'

Keith nodded.

He was in the middle of wondering whether he should remind her it was called growing when she suddenly scowled.

'Puppy fat,' she said, 'is not OK.'

She put her face close to Keith's.

Keith swallowed.

He noticed that one of her eyelashes was crooked.

Hope it's false, he thought.

'Do you know why puppy fat is not OK?' she asked.

Keith shook his head.

'Because,' she said, 'puppy fat doesn't always go away. Puppy fat can stay with you for the rest of your life.'

Keith thought about this.

'So what?' he asked.

'So what?' shouted Aunty Bev. 'So what?'

Keith's left buttock felt like it was going to run out the door on its own.

The chocolate fingers grabbed his guts and twisted.

But he found himself thinking of all the happy people he knew who weren't thin. Mr Gambaso in the Orchid Cove milkbar and the bloke who'd sold him the sugar cane and Ronnie Barker and the woman in the twenty-seven million quid painting.

'Yes,' shouted Keith. 'So what?'

'Keith!' boomed Dad's angry voice from the kitchen. 'Don't you ever talk to Bev like that again!'

Keith sighed.

He braced himself for the combined sight of Dad's angry red face and his spiky short haircut.

He heard Dad striding out of the kitchen and turned and started to explain that he hadn't meant to be rude but you have to be firm when you're arguing with a fanatic.

He didn't finish.

Dad's face wasn't red, it was shiny white.

His whole face was covered with white slime.

Stuck to the slime, beneath each eye,

was a slice of cucumber.

Keith stared.

Then he saw that Dad was holding a large pot of yoghurt.

Dad went over to Aunty Bev and put a protective arm round her shoulders.

'Did you hear what I said, Keith?' boomed Dad.

Keith managed to nod.

'Leave the cucumber over your eyes, Vin,' said Aunty Bev, slipping her arm round Dad's waist, 'or it won't absorb the muck from your eye sockets. It's OK, me and Keith were just having a bit of a debate, weren't we love?'

Keith tried to nod again but his neck had stopped working.

All he could do was stare in horror as Dad and Aunty Bev stood there with their arms round each other and Aunty Bev didn't even mind the yoghurt getting on her tracksuit.

$$*\qquad*\qquad*$$

'Thanks for trying,' said Tracy.

'That's OK,' said Keith.

They toyed listlessly with their

bacon, egg, sausage, onion and baked bean sandwiches.

'Do you think they'll get married?' asked Tracy.

'Dunno,' said Keith numbly.

He didn't even want to think about it.

Aunty Bev as a stepmother.

Bursting into his room checking he wasn't eating the tinned apricots.

Not that I'd have any appetite with her in the family, he thought gloomily.

'Perhaps,' said Tracy, 'falling in love will make her more relaxed about things.'

Keith looked at Tracy.

He could see she was just trying to cheer them both up, but it felt good all the same.

'Perhaps,' he said quietly.

Then the kitchen door flew open and Aunty Bev stood there looking at them both.

'G'day,' she said. 'Thought I'd find you in here.'

Tracy looked away.

Dazzle growled.

Keith gaped.

151

Underneath the tight fabric of Aunty Bev's pink tracksuit her stomach bulged out even further than Dad's.

No, he thought, it's not possible. She and Dad can't be having a baby already, not when she's only been in the country nine days.

'It's a cushion,' said Tracy wearily. 'It's to remind me that if I eat too much I'll get fat.'

'Good girl,' smiled Aunty Bev. 'You're getting the message.' She turned to Keith. 'And I hope you are too, young man. Short people have to be extra careful about their weight.'

Once they were alone again, Keith gave Tracy's arm a sympathetic squeeze.

'Oh, well,' he said, 'at least you've got Nepal to look forward to.'

Tracy shook her head.

'I'm not going,' she said quietly. 'Not even the highest mountains in the world are worth another week of this. Anyway, Aunty Bev reckons she's gunna stay on here with your dad for a bit and I've got to fly home by myself.'

Keith watched miserably as Tracy

dabbed her tears with her sandwich.

He had a vision of his life in London with Aunty Bev ruining most meals by nagging, and Dad ruining the rest by wearing yoghurt to the table.

He had a vision of Tracy's life in Australia, self-confidence shattered, hiding away by herself, pining for Nepal and watching telly and eating chocolate fingers and probably dying a lonely death tragically young.

It's all my fault, he thought.

Everything.

Then he knew what he had to do.

*   *   *

While he rummaged through Aunty Bev's suitcase he sent her a message.

Sorry to be going through your things, but Tracy needs someone to go with her to Nepal and then perk her up back in Australia, and as you're staying here now I'm going to use your ticket.

That's if I can find it, he thought.

He put the bras and tracksuits back into the suitcase and knelt down and opened the zip-up bag.

153

Shoes and a camera, but no plane ticket.

There was only the make-up bag to go.

Keith sent an urgent message to the ticket.

Please be in there.

I need you.

The bedroom door creaked and slowly started to open.

Keith froze.

Aunty Bev and Tracy couldn't be back from the newsagent already. It was a good ten minutes each way and that didn't include actually buying Tracy's diet book.

The door swung open and Dazzle trotted in.

He put his paws on Keith's chest and licked his face.

Keith started breathing again and gave Dazzle a hug.

'Don't worry,' he said, 'you're coming with me and Tracy.'

He opened the make-up bag.

A jolt of excitement ran through him.

Lying on top of the bottles and jars

was a plastic travel wallet.

He picked it up, hands shaking.

Inside was a passport and some Australian money and some duty free vouchers.

And a plane ticket.

Keith pulled the ticket out of the wallet.

His shoulders slumped.

Aunty Bev's name was in computer print.

That's it, thought Keith, sick with disappointment. Forget it.

You can change handwriting, but not computer print.

He was about to put the ticket back when he noticed something had fallen out of the wallet.

A photo.

A faded, tattered photo of a girl about Tracy's age in a swimming costume, with plump arms and stocky legs and a round body and a chubby face.

Aunty Bev's face.

CHAPTER FIFTEEN

'It's definitely her,' said Tracy. 'See that badge on her swimmers? That's the school she went to.'

Keith waited for his heart to stop thumping.

He realized it wasn't going to so he carried on anyway.

'You're dead sure?' he said.

'I'd bet my dad's crutches on it,' said Tracy. 'That dunny she's standing in front of was my grandma's.'

They crouched in the phone box and stared at the photo for a long time.

Keith's mind was racing and he could tell from Tracy's frown that hers probably was too.

After a while he slid the photo inside his jacket.

'I'm going to put it back before Mum gets home from work,' he said.

'Why?' asked Tracy. 'Why don't we go to the cafe and give Aunty Bev a squiz and remind her she used to be a normal kid so she'll leave me alone?'

'Cause if she's carrying this round with her,' said Keith, 'she doesn't need to be reminded.'

Tracy's face fell.

'Don't worry,' said Keith. 'I've got a better idea.'

*   *   *

Keith stood outside Mum's bathroom door and made sure he had a firm grip on his sketch pad and his nerves.

He could hear water splashing and the Beach Boys singing.

He sent an urgent message to the batteries in Mum's radio.

Just five more minutes, please. Last time if you'd conked out I'd have been sent to my room. This time I could go to jail.

Then he slowly turned the door handle and eased the door open a fraction.

He held his breath and hoped Aunty Bev couldn't hear the blood pounding in his ears.

She didn't seem to be able to.

She was lying back in the bath, eyes

closed, waving a sponge in time to the music.

Just stay like that for five minutes, begged Keith. Please.

He peered through the steam and started sketching.

Suddenly Aunty Bev started screaming.

Keith slammed the door and ran out of the flat and down the street to the police station, and explained frantically to the sergeant that he hadn't been sketching her rude bits, just her face.

That's what he did in his mind.

Before his body could follow along, he realized Aunty Bev was just singing.

He breathed a sigh of relief as quietly as he could and carried on sketching.

*   *   *

'Try and hold the torch steadier,' whispered Keith.

'Sorry,' said Tracy. 'It's this ladder, it's not designed for two people.'

Keith sighed to himself.

Bet the great painters of history

didn't have to do their best work in pitch darkness up Mitch Wilson's dad's gardening ladder with only a wobbly torch to see by.

Bet when Michelangelo made alterations to the mural in the Sistine Chapel he had scaffolding and floodlights.

Well, big candles anyway.

Plus he probably had more than the leftover Pond Green and Contemporary Beige from Dad's flat to work with.

'How's the torch now?' asked Tracy.

'Perfect, thanks,' said Keith, mixing up some more grey and brushing it on to the wall.

Then again, he thought, Michel-angelo probably didn't have his best mate to help him.

Keith leant back and looked at the expanse of mural in front of him.

That was Mum and Dad painted over.

Now to start on Aunty Bev.

*　　　*　　　*

'I still think this suit's too tight,' said Dad, puffing at the legs as he stepped off the kerb.

'No it's not,' said Aunty Bev. 'It'll be fine once you've sculpted your body profile. Plus that fabric'll stretch with wear. Take bigger steps.'

Dad took bigger steps as they crossed the road, but Keith could see he wasn't happy.

Keith wasn't happy either.

He sent Dad an urgent message.

Don't worry about the new suit now, please, it'll distract Aunty Bev from the mural.

Keith glanced at Tracy and could see from her tense face that she was worried about the same thing.

Dad pulled at the sleeves of the suit.

'The mural's just round this corner,' said Keith.

'This is very exciting,' said Aunty Bev. 'Why didn't you tell me about it before?'

'Keith's a bit nervous about his paintings,' said Tracy. 'He's worried that people won't understand them.'

Keith and Tracy exchanged a glance

and Keith saw that her fingers were crossed as tightly as his.

He held his breath as they turned the corner.

'Jeez,' said Aunty Bev, staring up at the mural. 'Look at the size of it.'

For a horrible moment Keith thought she meant the body of the attractive and stylish Contemporary Beige woman with the Pond Green swimsuit and the plump arms and the stocky legs and the round body and the chubby face which, Keith was relieved to see, even in daylight was a pretty good likeness of Aunty Bev.

But she didn't.

'The colours on the houses are fabulous,' said Aunty Bev.

'What happened to the weight-lifters?' said Dad with a puzzled frown.

'I changed it,' said Keith quietly.

Please, he begged Aunty Bev silently, please do us all a favour and recognize your real self and feel OK about it.

Aunty Bev stared at herself on the wall.

Keith's heart thumped with excitement.

Aunty Bev turned to Tracy.

'That's exactly what I've been trying to tell you,' she said, pointing up at the woman. 'Puppy fat can stay with you and ruin your life.'

Then she turned to Dad.

'On second thoughts,' she said, 'I think that suit is too tight.'

* * *

Keith's feet hurt.

Not surprisingly, he thought gloomily, I must have walked hundreds of miles.

He walked a bit more, then it hit him that if his feet hurt, Dazzle's probably did too.

He picked Dazzle up and tucked the panting dog inside his jacket.

'Sorry,' he said.

Dazzle licked his chin.

Under the next street light Keith looked at his watch, but it had stopped.

Dad and Aunty Bev were probably home from their visit to the doctor to see if Dad could get liposuction on the Government and were probably wondering where he was.

Tracy had probably slept off her headache and was probably wondering where he was too.

Keith realized he didn't know where he was.

He peered around but the dark houses all looked the same.

Serves me right if I'm lost for ever, thought Keith gloomily. A person who ruins his dad's life and his best friend's life and can't even fix things up with a two hundred square-foot mural deserves to be lost.

Dazzle started to wail softly.

Keith patted his head.

'Don't be upset,' he said, 'we're not really lost. We're somewhere in South London.'

Dazzle kept on wailing.

He knows, thought Keith, he knows we won't be able to stay in South London with Aunty Bev here.

And suddenly Keith wanted to wail himself.

He wanted to snuggle inside Mum's jacket, or Dad's, and tell them how scared and unhappy he was.

He looked around for a street sign to help him get home, but all he could see was a gatepost.

A gatepost with a jagged slash of new wood on it.

Mr Mellish's gatepost.

Dazzle's wails got louder and Keith suddenly knew why.

'He's gone,' he said softly to the trembling dog. 'There's nothing you can do.'

Keith felt wetness on his hand.

You poor little thing, he thought, you're crying.

Then Keith realized the tears weren't Dazzle's, they were his.

*   *   *

Please be home, Mum, thought Keith as he softly closed the door.

As his eyes got used to the darkness he saw that Mum's bed on the settee was empty.

Then he heard it.

The quiet sobbing coming from the bathroom.

Oh no, he thought, I knew it was too

good to be true.

I knew it was too much to hope that Mum and Donald could find happiness together what with them both being parking inspectors and under so much stress.

And now they've split up.

Poor Mum.

Keith knocked softly on the bathroom door, then pushed it open.

He could just make out a figure sitting on the edge of the bath in a dressing gown, shaking with sobs.

'Don't sit there in the dark,' he said softly, and put the light on.

Aunty Bev blinked at him with red-rimmed eyes.

Keith blinked back.

He saw she was holding the tattered photo of herself as a kid in one hand and a half-empty packet of chocolate fingers in the other.

'Sorry,' said Keith.

'That's OK,' said Aunty Bev. 'I'm just feeling a bit weepy.'

She looked at the photo, then at the chocolate fingers.

'Can I tell you something just

between us?' she said.

'Yes,' said Keith, hoping desperately she wasn't going to lecture him about how eating chocolate fingers would give him puppy fat.

'It's not going to work with me and your dad,' she said sadly. 'He thinks I nag him too much.'

'Oh,' said Keith.

Aunty Bev put a chocolate finger into her mouth.

'I haven't had a chocolate finger for nineteen years,' she said.

'That must have been awful,' said Keith.

Aunty Bev wiped her nose on the back of her hand. 'It's not a lot of fun,' she said, 'staying thin and beautiful.'

Keith wondered if he should let her know she looked nicer with red eyes and a brown mouth.

'Do you know what I've always wanted to do for my holidays?' said Aunty Bev.

'Go to Nepal?' said Keith.

'Spend two weeks with a normal tummy like your dad and comfy hair like your mum,' said Aunty Bev.

'Why don't you?' said Keith.

CHAPTER SIXTEEN

Keith stumbled downstairs to the cafe, rubbing his eyes, Dazzle panting at his heels.

That, he thought, was the best sleep I've had in months.

Then he stopped.

Something was wrong.

Why couldn't he smell frying?

It was after midday and Tracy and Aunty Bev would be arriving for Sunday lunch any sec and Dad should have been well into cooking the fish and chips.

Then he saw Dad sitting at one of the tables in his Simpsons T-shirt and baggy old trousers, shoulders slumped, staring into a cuppa.

'You all right Dad?' he said.

'Fine,' said Dad, looking up and trying to smile.

'Dad,' said Keith quietly, 'is it Aunty Bev?'

Dad stared into his cuppa.

'Son,' he said after a bit, 'can I tell you something just between us?'

'Yes,' said Keith.

'It's not going to work out between me and Bev,' said Dad softly. 'She wants someone thin and good-looking.'

Keith sat down at the table, heart pounding, and started sorting out in his mind all the things he had to tell Dad.

How Aunty Bev had discovered her real self.

How she wouldn't be nagging anyone any more.

How Dad and her could fall in love and have a long and happy life together in comfy clothes.

Keith opened his mouth, but before he could start Aunty Bev's voice rang out from the doorway.

'G'day Vin, g'day Keith.'

Keith kept his eyes on Dad's face, waiting for Dad's reaction when he saw what Bev was wearing. One of Mum's baggy old tracksuits probably and a pair of her sensible shoes and flat hair and no make-up.

Keith waited.

168

'Hello Bev, hello Tracy,' said Dad, face still serious.

Keith waited some more.

Oh no, he thought, Dad's eyes really have gone this time.

Keith turned round.

His stomach sagged.

Aunty Bev was wearing her tight pink tracksuit and her shiny red shoes and her hair was bouncing gently around her perfectly made-up face.

'Sorry,' said Dad, standing up, 'I'm a bit behind with lunch.'

'No worries,' said Aunty Bev. 'Won't hurt Tracy to wait a bit. We won't be eating much in Nepal so she might as well get used to it now.'

Keith looked sadly at Tracy.

Poor thing, he thought.

Tracy turned to Aunty Bev.

'You can wait if you want,' she said, 'but I'm starving.'

'Eh?' said Aunty Bev.

Keith stared.

'Come on,' said Tracy, 'let's all get stuck in and help.'

* * *

Keith didn't get a chance to speak to Tracy in private until they were at the sink together peeling the potatoes.

'Good one,' he said.

'Thanks,' said Tracy.

'How did you do it?' he said.

'It was easy,' replied Tracy. 'I just have to remember she's not really nagging me, she's nagging herself.'

Keith looked at her happily.

Good old Tracy, he thought. Wish I was as quick as her at catching the drift.

He took a deep breath.

Now for the tricky bit.

'Sorry,' he said.

Tracy finished scraping the eye out of a potato and gave him a long look.

She didn't say anything.

Keith took another deep breath.

'Sorry I've spent most of your trip being a wally,' he said.

Tracy grinned. 'You mean a prawn.'

'Yeah,' he said.

'You weren't,' she said. 'Though I did think I'd lost a best mate there, for a bit.'

Everyone at the airport looked like they'd just got off a long flight, even the people who hadn't started theirs yet.

Except Aunty Bev.

Keith decided to give Tracy her present now so Aunty Bev could get used to it and not throw a tizz on the plane and perhaps pierce the fuselage with her high heels.

'Here,' he said to Tracy, 'this is for you.'

'Ripper,' said Tracy, opening the bag and taking out the four egg, bacon, sausage, onion and Vegemite rolls. 'These'll keep me going all the way to Nepal. Thanks.'

Keith saw Aunty Bev's lips tighten.

'It's OK,' Tracy said to her, 'I'll walk around the plane while I'm eating them.'

Before Aunty Bev could say anything, their flight was announced.

Aunty Bev and Dad shook hands, then kissed each other on the cheek.

Keith and Tracy hugged each other, and Dazzle licked Tracy on the face.

'I'm going to miss you,' said Keith.

'I'm gunna miss you too,' said Tracy. 'How many plates was it you have to wash up to pay for a ticket to Australia?'

'Eighteen thousand,' said Keith.

'Think positive,' said Tracy.

Keith grinned.

While Dad and Tracy were saying goodbye, Aunty Bev gave Keith a quick hug, then glanced around to make sure nobody could hear her.

'You're a good painter,' she said quietly, 'keep at it.'

As Tracy and Aunty Bev walked through the departure gate, Keith sent Tracy an urgent message. Stay in touch.

This is daft, he thought, the problem with silent messages is you never know if they've got through.

'Stay in touch,' he called.

Tracy stopped and turned and grinned at him.

'No worries,' she said. 'Best mates always do.'

172

CHAPTER SEVENTEEN

'Nice,' said Mr Dodd, looking up at the wall. 'Very nice.'

'Hope it sells some paint,' said Keith, wiping his hands on a rag.

'Can't miss,' said Mr Dodd, 'not with lettering that big.'

'Hmmmnm,' said a voice behind Keith.

Keith turned.

It was Mr Browning.

' "Dodds Hardware For All Your Paint Needs",' read Mr Browning. ' "Expert Advice. Rock Bottom Prices." Very effective. I particularly like the contrast between the blue background and the ochre lettering.'

'It's Suntan Gold actually,' said Mr Dodd.

'Pity about the mural though,' said Mr Browning, 'it was very good.'

'I liked the second version best,' said Mr Dodd. 'That well-built woman in the Pond Green swimsuit.'

'They were both fine examples of

non-realist art,' said Mr Browning.

You're right there, thought Keith, smiling to himself. They were a bit unrealistic.

After Mr Browning had gone, Mr Dodd invited Keith into the shop for a drink and a cake.

'Thanks,' said Keith, 'but I'm a bit pressed for time. I've got to organize an art exhibition.'

*   *   *

After Keith declared the art exhibition open, he handed round tea and chocolate fingers.

It didn't take long because there were only two people at the viewing.

'Nice tea,' said Dad.

'Yummy chocolate fingers,' said Mum.

Then they talked with the artist about his work.

Keith explained that the two paintings used to be one, but he'd cut it in half so they could each have their own bit.

'Yours is called *Nude Dad With*

Frying Pan,' he told Dad. 'Don't touch the bald patch, it's still a bit wet.'

'It's brilliantly life-like,' said Dad. 'You've got my saggy tummy and wobbly bottom down to a T.'

'Art should be truthful,' said Keith.

He told Mum the title of hers.

'*Venus Soaking Her Corns,*' she grinned. 'I like it, though it should really be called *Venus Soaking Her Corns and Droopy Shoulders.*'

Keith explained about the shower curtain, and offered to paint it back in, but Mum said what was good enough for Rembrandt's models was good enough for her.

Then it was time for Dad to go to the cafe and Mum to go and meet Donald at the pictures.

They each took their painting, and thanked him so much that by the time they'd finished he felt about six pineapple boxes tall.

They both put their arms round him and gave him a hug.

Funny, thought Keith, they both seem a bit shorter than the last time we did this.

Perhaps they're shrinking with old age.

Then another possibility hit him.

He ran into Mum's bathroom and stood in front of the mirror, guts tingling with happiness.

His face beamed back at him, grin included.

Keith wondered if he should send a message to the chicken nuggets and peas in his stomach. Let them know it wasn't a big drama, he was just excited to be growing again.

No, he decided, I won't. They're big chicken nuggets and peas and they can look after themselves.